Cold Wind in Alaska

Elaine Waldron

A Symes-Mobberley House Publication

Chapter One

The caustic, reverberating-ring of the big off-white alarm clock went off at nine am, sending Lois Williams tumbling out of bed and grumbling short spurts of obscenities, while hitting the floor with a thud, landing on her rear. One might as well have blown a trumpet in her ear. She really loathed that ugly clock. But her husband, Doug, refused to replace it, saying it was the only alarm that ever worked in waking him up.

She'd been in a well-needed deep sleep, as she hadn't slept at all the previous night, having done what she knew better than to do. She'd had a cup of coffee after nine pm. Painfully wide awake now and sitting up in an unattractive position in the floor, she swore some more, untangled her ankles from the ends of the white sheet, tossed them back on the bed and, after struggling into her red-and-black-checkered robe (which really belonged to her six-foot-four husband), and her furry black slippers, she made her way into the kitchen. She rinsed out the four-cup glass pot and filled it with water from the tap, placed the pot on the warmer, then took fresh coffee and filled the filter halfway to the top (she preferred her coffee strong), closed the lid, and switched the maker on. She then plopped down on the ladder-backed chair at the side of the small kitchen table Doug had built from scrap wood.

It was just her, Doug, and a whole slew of dogs, primarily Alaskan Huskies. No kids, and living in the wilds of Alaska, rarely did they have company. The small table was all that was needed. But, damn, if she didn't miss Doug when he was gone, even when it was just to pick up supplies.

Coffee finished, she poured herself a mug full and ambled into their small living room. The fire had gone out in the hearth. "Brrrr..." she said, shivering hard, questioning her sanity for having married a law-enforcement park ranger. He'd warned her Alaska would be cold. She just hadn't realized *how* cold. Noticing that there were still a few glowing cinders in the fireplace, she stirred them up and tossed in a few small pieces of kindling. To her relief, it caught. She then tossed in a couple of logs, placed the screen back in front of the fire, and sat on the sofa to finish her coffee before it cooled off. She'd always found the snapping and crackling of fire in the hearth pleasant and never tired of it.

There was a scratching at the front door – Nikki – her Samoyed, a wedding gift from Doug. She'd almost forgotten about him, even when Doug had left at four am. Nikki had probably still been wandering around outside then and not yet ready to come in. He'd wanted out in the middle of the night and she'd gone back to bed after letting him out. She set her mug aside on the end table and let him in. First thing he did was shake the loose snow off his heavy, pure-white pelt, showering droplets everywhere. But Lois didn't mind much. After all, it was a log cabin with just a bare wood floor and braided rugs scattered here and there. Doug's mom, who lived in Ontario, had made them. "Morning, Nikki," she said to the dog. He woofed as though answering, and headed straight for his big blue bowl in the kitchen, which was just to the right of the small refrigerator. The team dogs were fed outside.

The bowl was nearly empty. He stared intently at her with obsidian eyes and woofed again. "Okay... okay... don't get your dander up. I'm gonna feed you."

Her mug was empty anyway, and though she'd had plenty of coffee, she still craved more. But first, she scooped up several cups of Purina from the fifty pound sack that was by the back door into Nikki's bowl, then filled her mug with more coffee and returned to the living room to sit in front of and relish the fire. The wind outside had picked up and had started to whistle through the door. Not good. Not good at all. Now she was really becoming concerned for Doug. She rose and went over to the window. The snow was falling in huge flakes. "Crap!" It crossed her mind that the blizzard was coming in earlier than expected, Doug might have to buckle down somewhere, and she'd be stuck there alone. "Dammit! Why'd you have to go this time? You knew it was risky?" But she knew she was speaking only to the walls of the cabin and her dog. She returned to the sofa and made herself focus on drinking her coffee and enjoying the flames in the hearth.

Around one pm Lois was really beginning to get anxious about her husband. He was only about two hours late in getting home, nothing unusual, it had happened often. Still, she worried. There was little she could do, if he didn't show either. Winter was setting in fast and hard. She'd tried to talk Doug out of making this last trip before the blizzard blew in, but he insisted they still needed a few more supplies. She knew he really just wanted an excuse to exercise his dogs. There was no reason he couldn't have taken the heavy-duty pickup that he used for his job as a law-enforcement ranger.

There was no television reception where they were. But they had a television and a DVD player, lots of movies on DVD and a Ham radio. She sat down in front of the radio and called in to the ranger station. Joe Welch, a senior park ranger and one of the region's big bosses that came in every few weeks or so to see how things were going (his main office was in Anchorage) answered instead of Billy Phillips, surprising her somewhat, as Billy normally answered that time of morning. Said all was fine there, but the blizzard had definitely arrived. To her relief, though, he did say Doug had dropped in at the station after shopping and that he was now on his way home and should be arriving soon. That he, himself, was just getting ready to head back to Anchorage. She thanked him, but knew she wouldn't be completely relieved until Doug was home.

Doug Williams cursed under his breath. Big white flakes swirled in sheets so hard he could barely see. The dogs were anxious, and sensed his frustration. He should have listened to Lois and taken his heavy duty-pickup into Cold Town. He would have gotten back before the storm blew in. The snow had been perfect, though, and he liked to take the dogs out at least once a month when the weather was right, to keep them and his self in shape. They had been low on staples. And staples were something one couldn't do without during the long winters. He, especially, didn't want his wife running out if he were to get stuck out in the wilderness somewhere and unable to get back for a few days.

There was plenty of meat in the smokehouse and freezer, but flour, salt, rice, beans, the things that kept you going through the extreme cold days and nights had been low. Now...all he had to do was get them home. And it wasn't that far. But visibility was very bad. He could hardly see his dogs in front. And the drifts were high and getting higher. "Should have listened to Lois," he said. "No...Should have bought the staples last time we were in town when she suggested we do so."

The dogs slowed down, for the snow was deepening so fast it was piling up right in their path. They could handle it, just took them longer to get through. The lead dog, Nook, woofed and struggled hard to encourage the others.

"Just a little further, Nook," Doug yelled. "Just a little further." Suddenly, he noticed something darkening the sky ahead, something drifting high – smoke! Smoke from their cabin. "Yes! That's it, Nook. We're there!"

Nook definitely understood, as well as the rest of the pack, and they lunged forward at once with a renewed energy and all but flew down the slope and came to a sliding stop in front of the cabin. "Finally!" Doug said, stepping down. "And thank you, God," he said aloud. "Thank you for saving me from my stubborn stupidity." He began unloading the supplies.

Lois heard the excited barking and yipping of dogs and ran out, Nikki at her side. She greeted her husband with a kiss on the cheek, but scolded him at the same time for having gone at all.

"What can I say, Lois," he commented with an endearing smile, revealing his deep dimples that could set her heart to racing, and handed her a twenty pound bag of rice to carry in. He hoisted an even larger bag of pinto beans over one shoulder and a twenty pound bag of flour over the other, and then followed her inside. Soon they were in the cabin, dogs included (after they were unhitched and fed). Doug and his team – including Nikki, who was glad to see them – crowded around in front of the hearth to dry off while Lois went to the kitchen to make her husband something to eat.

Later that evening, they talked for several hours and then made love in the warmth of their bedroom while the walls moaned and creaked and the winds relentlessly howled outside. Nikki and Nook, an Alaskan malamute with keen blue eyes and the lead dog, lay just at the foot of their bed. The other dogs stayed curled up by the fire in the living room. It was times like these, when all snuggled up near her husband, that Lois felt that dealing with the cold and living in the wilderness was more than worth it. Just being with Doug seemed sheer paradise. He was a good man, had a good heart. And he loved it here. She loved it, too, though not as much as he.

She would have preferred being a little closer to civilization. It would have made life a little easier. And he had promised her, that if any children ever came along, he would put in for a transfer so they could live nearer some semblance of civilization, possibly in the Seattle area, which could potentially mean giving up most of his dogs. She knew, deep down, that that was something that would be really hard for him to do. She knew he'd keep his promise, though, if she persisted, but she wasn't sure she could do that to him. And she trusted him completely. Otherwise, she would not have married him and made the huge step of leaving her mother, her sister, Sally, and home in Seattle and moving here to this obscure little cabin in the Alaskan wilderness. But he was a park ranger, had been for fifteen years, and had no inclination to be anything else. It was in his blood, as he sometimes reminded her.

They'd met in Seattle one night at a birthday party for her girlfriend, Gloria Williams – they'd become friends their last year of college – and it turned out that Doug was Gloria's brother, and he was home on a rare vacation. It was love at first sight. He'd virtually swept her off her feet. She'd been instantly attracted to his simple but refreshing honesty and his outdoors-man ways. They'd dated like mad for two weeks, a whirlwind relationship, and the next thing she knew, she'd forgotten all about becoming a nurse, married him in a quick ceremony in her mom's parish (while Sally and their mom gushed continuous tears), and was off for the life of a ranger's wife in this remote part of the Alaska Range she'd never heard of.

"This is BP1... Doug, you there? Over..." Billy Phillip's husky voice woke them with a start. "Doug... You there? Over..."

Doug scrambled out of bed and answered the call, "Roger that, BP...What's up? Over..."

"I hate to be the one to send bad news in after such rough weather... But we have a problem... Over."

"Roger. What's up? Over."

"Someone's shot and killed old man Clifford and his wife, Bell. Down at Clifford's Hardware and Supply... Happened about an hour ago. Over."

"Roger that! Christ sake! I was just there yesterday! Over."

Lois didn't like this at all. She was out of bed and had latched onto Doug's free arm. There was no way she wanted him to go out in the current weather conditions, though one glance out the window told her the snow had stopped for the moment, but she had a definite sinking feeling he was going to. When he signed off, he turned to her with that look of his, the one that said, "Sorry, babe...but this is a *have to!*"

"Dammit! Doug! Why does it always have to be you?"

"Because it's my job. You know that, babe. And this is Clifford and Bell!" Tears filled his eyes. "I just bought supplies from them yesterday morning!"

She turned away, not wanting to see him cry, and looked out at the snow on the window sills. "The snow's getting really deep out there, Doug. There's no way you're gonna get the truck through this!"

"I probably could. But it would be highly risky. But that's where my dogs come in, Lois," he said, gently taking her by her shoulders and making her turn back around.

Her eyes fell to Nook. His cool blue eyes stared back her as though to say, "It's okay, Lois. I have everything under control." But did he? He was probably one of the best lead dogs in Alaska... He'd led his team and Doug to win the Iditarod only two years before.

Doug interrupted her thoughts. "I have to do this, Lois. Chances of my catching this man are slim, as it is. And I'm sure Paul's working in from the east. We'll probably meet somewhere in between." He began changing into his uniform.

"Dammit! Doug!" She said, looking up into his beautiful hazel eyes, but knowing it was fruitless.

"Babe, I could use one of those Paul Bunyan breakfast's that you like to cook up for me. Pancakes...sausages...bacon...three eggs. You know... the works... coffee... orange juice. And I'll pack some of your homemade jerky and bread to take along with my regular rations." Making the jerky had been her first attempt at such things. But to Doug's happy surprise it had actually turned out really good, almost as good as his.

There was a deep melancholic sigh from her, but she turned, donned her robe and went to make his breakfast.

"That's my girl," Doug said, and finished strapping on his gun belt. Slipped his .45 in the holster, then got his high-powered rifle with optical sights out of the gun cabinet. He made sure he had plenty of ammo strapped on, and then went out to hook up the team.

Shelton Webb hadn't meant to kill the old codger and his wife. He'd just meant to take a few supplies and what little of the green stuff was in the register, as Jenny, his *wife*, and Fred Masters, his *best friend,* had taken off with all the money they'd swindled that poor old widow, Malerie Perkins, out of back in Wyoming – two hundred thousand dollars! Except the money for the room at the lodge and a couple of meals, they'd taken off with the entire load in the truck they'd stolen from Fred's ex's new husband, when the newlyweds were out of town on their honeymoon, leaving him with five dollars and a few quarters change in his pocket. Jenny had even cleaned his two credit cards out of his wallet when he wasn't looking.

It had been an instant decision. He's stepped outside the lodge and walked across the street to Supply & Hardware, which seemed to be the only store around that could have enough money to take the risk. He had stood outside the store shivering in his coat for almost twenty minutes, mustering up the courage to go inside. But, after thinking over his desperate situation, looking around and seeing how very stranded he was – except for Cold Town Lodge, Supply & Hardware, a clinic, and a small hotel, there wasn't much left but snow, ice and frozen range between mountains, peppered with trees. He'd pulled his collar up around his ears and his brown beanie down, almost covering his eyes, took a deep breath for courage and walked in the store, which looked deserted at that precise moment. He'd glanced around and thinking no one to be in the immediate surroundings, he quickly made his way behind the counter and over to the register, which he promptly opened – with a loud ring!

That was when the old man walked in.

After being caught with his hands in the register, a shouting match ensued and Shelton frantically tried to reason with the old man, did his best to explain that he only wanted enough cash to get away, that he'd even return the money once he got back home, but the owner was a stubborn old fool, raised up the shotgun he had in his hands and expected Shelton to stand there while he called the ranger's station. Likewise, Shelton had pulled out his .45 semi-automatic and ordered the old man to put the shotgun away. That was when all hell broke loose. For just then the old lady appeared out of seemingly nowhere, walking in with a .22 semi-automatic in her badly shaking hands and fired two shots, just missing his left shoulder and damn near hitting the old man. Shelton lost it then, reacting out of pure panic and reflex. He let them both have it, instantly killing the old man and his wife. He stood there momentarily, not believing what had happened and what he'd just done. *"Oh my God! This isn't happening!"*

Had the situation not been so tense, he realized it probably wouldn't have happened – He'd never killed anyone before. But one doesn't think clearly when they're being shot at. Now, here he was, a fugitive in more than one state, wanted for fraud, and now he'd added robbery and *murder*. What the hell was he gonna do? And where in hell was he gonna go?

He had thought clearly enough to take the keys to the old codger's heavy-duty pickup with a small plow on the front that he'd seen parked out back. But now the snow was piled so high, even the large pickup with its giant tires was having difficulty making its way through. He wondered why in hell anyone would want to live out here with these conditions.

Hell! He didn't even have a clue where he was going!

He wasn't familiar with Alaska. Didn't even know for sure where the road was supposed to be. Best he could remember it was the George Parks Highway. When he'd first started out, he could make it out, the road being level and somewhat smooth in comparison to the rest of the snow-covered landscape. Now, the white stuff had started in again, and all he could see was snow, snow and more snow. He was glad he had good sunglasses or he was sure he would have been snow-blind by now. He'd turned on the radio, and there was music for a while, country music. Now, there was nothing but static.

Shelton pushed the truck onward, winding this way and that in the deepening drifts across the road, hoping he'd find a place to get in out of the weather, a shed, anything, until the snow let up. (He'd tried to get the plow to work, but it seemed to be frozen up.) That is, if it was going to. From what he'd heard from some of the locals right before leaving the lodge lobby, it didn't sound so good for the next few days. Besides the blizzard coming in, another one was going to be directly behind it. The only consolation he had was in realizing that the truck his dear wife and "best friend" were in wasn't equipped for this kind of weather. He figured they were plowed into a snowdrift somewhere by now. If not, then they soon would be. "Serves 'em right!" he snarled. "Serves 'em right!"

Fred and Jenny had headed south on the George Parks Highway, headed for Anchorage, hoping to reach the more populated area before the weather got too bad, a blizzard had started up. Only they hadn't even made it a third of the way before visibility became nearly impossible.

"What are we gonna do?" Jenny asked, nervously chewing her fingernails and watching the snow heap up on the windshield. The wipers were working hard to push it away, but couldn't keep up with the accumulation anymore. For the first time in her life, she was actually a little scared. She'd done some questionable things in her time, but never anything like this. Shelton would surely come after them, and though he'd never killed anyone before, she did wonder if he would kill them if he got the chance. He did have a nasty temper when provoked. She figured he'd consider being betrayed and abandoned in a freezing hell a good reason for provocation. That wasn't her only concern, though. Were they ever going to get out of this terrible storm alive? "Are we even still on the road?"

"Dammit! Will you shut up, woman?" Fred snarled. He was doing his best to keep the truck on the road, but he was losing the battle. He tried to go through a high drift and the truck stopped. "Fuck!" He jumped out and went around to the rear of the pickup. He'd seen a snow shovel in the back. He dug for it and found it. There was another, smaller shovel, with it. He grabbed it, too. Then he opened the door and yelled at Jenny to get out and help him shovel the snow out of the way.

"What good's that gonna do?" she retorted, realizing their battle was probably fruitless.

"Just shut your trap and dig!" He began shoveling as fast as he could and managed to get a good heap of it out of the way. He tossed a sharp look her way. She wasn't doing much good, if any. "Get in. We'll try it again."

They jumped in and he threw the truck in reverse first, glad it was a stick, then threw it in low gear and stepped on the gas. The tires spun for a moment and then caught. "Whoopie!" he yelled as they broke through the drift. He glanced over at her. "We'll make it, woman. You'll see."

"I hope so," was all she said.

He snarled in canine manner, very irritated with her lack of faith in him, but kept his eyes on the road, trying to not let her get under his skin. After all, they'd just run out on her husband and his best friend. He hoped he'd not screwed up. "Love me, woman?"

She didn't answer.

"Love me?" he said a lot louder.

Her eyes blinked and she turned her face to him. "Yes! Of course, I do. I wouldn't be here and taking this crazy chance, if I didn't."

"I sure hope you're telling me the truth. Otherwise, it could be a real pisser of a relationship. Things could get real unpleasant."

A dark look crossed her face. "Are you... threatening me, Fred?"

He snickered slightly and smiled wryly. "Of course not. I just meant that we're not gonna be really happy with one another, if you don't love me. After all, Shelton *was* my best friend."

"And my husband!"

"And don't forget the money. Now it's a two-way split. Not three."

She thought for a moment and then smiled. "Yeah. Almost a hundred thousand a piece.

He reflected her smile and patted her thigh. "That's more like it, woman. Keep smiling. We're gonna make it through this. You'll see."

"Yes, Fred. We're gonna make it," she replied, but she wasn't so sure when she looked at the washboard-ridged road and the blinding white stuff blowing in sheets across their path.

Lois, realizing it was going to be a long day, possibly even turning into several days, decided she wasn't doing herself any favors in feeding her depression by sulking around. She might as well do her best to keep busy. She'd brought in a shoulder roast from the freezer on the back porch, laughing at the irony of having meat in the freezer when so much of the time the temperatures here were below freezing, and placed it in the microwave to thaw out. There was more meat in the smokehouse (Doug had checked on the slow-burning fire before leaving to make sure it wouldn't got out) mostly venison, but he would have to cut it up before it could be used, it was hanging in shanks, much too big for her to fool with.

Ready now to start preparing her stew, she took the meat out of the microwave, rinsed it off, as it was now oozing drops of blood from being thawed out, and laid it in the sink and cut it up into bite-sized chunks, rinsed them off and tossed them into the cast-iron pot. She had modern cookware if she wanted to use it, but preferred cooking most things in cast-iron. For one reason, she knew it helped in keeping the iron levels in the blood good, without having to take any supplements. Something she'd learned from her mother who, as a young woman, had learned it from her mother. She then tossed in chunks of carrots, onions, Lima beans and celery. She would wait until the stew was almost done before adding the potatoes. She didn't like her potatoes mushy, wanted something to bite into and not have it disintegrate in her mouth when eating. Stew on, she set about preparing dough for homemade bread. She was sure it would have plenty of time to rise before baking.

Having finished in the kitchen, she fed Nikki and then grabbed a couple of books off the shelf; one Doug had bought for her a few weeks back. It was *Isaac Asimov Gold: The Final Science Fiction Collection.* She loved science fiction and Asimov was her second favorite author. Her favorite writer was John W. Cassell. She'd read his *Crossroads* 1969 and now had a new copy of *Soldier of Aquarius 1969-1970* that she'd had her mother order from Barnes & Noble. It had come just that past week. She was saving it for last. She stoked up the flames in the fireplace and settled down on the sofa to read. It was three in the afternoon now, but she didn't care. Time wasn't a problem on these winter days, especially when Doug wasn't home. She was glad he'd made sure the generator had plenty of fuel before he left. It would be good now for several days. At least, she didn't have to worry about trudging out into the snow to refuel it. Surely he'd be home before that needed to be done.

Nikki finished eating, padded in and, after nudging her affectionately in the ribs with his cold wet nose, made himself comfortable at her feet and quickly fell to sleep. "Sounds like a good idea to me," she said looking down at the dog. "Think I'll try a short nap, too." She set her open-faced book aside on the end table, and stretched out across the sofa, covering herself with her red and white checkerboard quilt, one of many wedding gifts from her mother, and closed her eyes. The fire under the stew was turned very low; it could simmer that way for hours before she needed to worry about it. She dropped off into slumber almost immediately.

Chapter Two

Thirty-seven-year-old Ranger Paul Bates, slowly inched his 2004 Suburban down the road that was covered in a washboard pattern of snow. He wasn't one to give up, but was quickly coming to the realization that he might be going back to hitch up his dogs and sled, which he was pretty sure his friend, Doug, had already done. Doug, in fact, most likely hadn't even bothered with his truck, needing little excuse in taking his dogs out. Paul, on the other hand, wasn't as much into mushing as his friend. He preferred the comforts of his sports utility vehicle when the weather was this cold. Only, these heavy-duty vehicles still couldn't get through everything. He'd been hoping, though.

Up ahead, Paul noticed a red Ford pickup stuck off the side of the road, angling sideways, grill facing the road. The driver was doing his damn best to ruin his tires, spinning them for all they were worth, trying to get out and back on the road. "Idiot," he said under his breath. He moved his vehicle along slowly. "Worst thing he can do... Obviously, not from around here." He knew then that this could possibly be the person or persons he was looking for. He approached with caution. When the man inside saw him, he jumped out and started waving in scissors fashion. Paul eased up as close as he could without getting off the road, took a minute to call in to the station, and then got out. By then, there was a redheaded woman with a blue blanket wrapped around her body over a brown suede coat, standing beside the man, looking very cold and upset.

"Are we glad to see you!" the woman shouted over the howling wind.

Paul pulled the fur-lined collar of his coat up and trudged over to them in the crunchy snow. "From the looks of things," he said, "your truck isn't going anywhere for awhile."

"Yeah..." the man replied in a nervous voice. "I kind of figured that. But I had no idea anyone would be coming along anytime soon."

"You're just lucky I was out this way," Paul said. "Otherwise, you'd most likely be correct in that assumption." Paul didn't like the shifty-eyed man. The woman looked like she was hiding something, too. In spite of the fact that she looked very cold, she was almost smiling, as though harboring some wonderful secret. He was good at masking his thoughts, though, from ten years of experience. "Not from around here... I take it."

"Got that right," Jenny replied. "We're from Wyoming."

Paul instantly knew that was a lie, though the license plate did say Wyoming. If they were really from there, they would have known better than to try and take an unequipped truck, which looked brand new, on the road in these extreme conditions. In fact, they wouldn't have done it. Definitely something amiss here, but he wasn't so sure they were who he was looking for. They could be just a couple of greenhorn tourists having come at a bad time.

Paul made his way around the truck, taking in the situation. "Well, the best I can do for you fine folks is give you a lift into to the lodge in town. You'll have to get your truck later, when the weather permits...From what I understand, it's supposed to let up in a little bit with spells in between. Then there's the probability of another storm coming our way. Maybe in the breaks the roads can be cleared off enough for Joe Screaming Chicken to pull you out...He's the town mechanic and also does all the towing around here.

The man and woman glanced at one another. There was something they weren't telling him. "We just left the lodge this morning," the man informed him.

"Well, I can't leave you out here," Paul said. "Climb in my Suburban and I'll give you a lift. The only other alternative is to take you to the station, but we don't have facilities for guests. I think the lodge is about the only choice. There's a small hotel of about six rooms, but I think it's packed. Some other good folks like you got themselves caught up in this storm, too."

There was an odd expression on Fred's face, but he finally said okay, but asked Paul to wait a minute. He wanted to grab some things out of his truck. Paul nodded it was okay. Just then, he heard a call coming over his radio in the Suburban, sounded like Doug, and there was an urgent tone to his voice. Then Paul did what he really knew better than to do, but it was really cold and he wanted to get these people out of the weather as soon as possible, and he took this one chance – He turned his back on the two strangers and went to answer the call – But swung around when he heard the woman shout, *"Fred!"* It was too late. The man fired the double-barreled shotgun straight on. The look on Paul's face was of total shock, just before he dropped dead into the snow.

"What the hell did you do that for?" Jenny shrieked unbelievingly. *"Oh my God! Oh my God!"*

Fred yelled for her to shut her trap. "Had no choice, Jenny. We couldn't chance letting him take us back to the lodge or the station... or answering that call. It could have been about us. Either way, we would have been found out... for stealing the truck, and Shelton could still be there. Crap! Had no choice! Besides," he indicated with a nod, "the ranger's Suburban might get us outta here."

"There are markings on the side. You're not a law-enforcement ranger, Fred. We'll get caught for sure in his ride."

"We'll take it as far as we can, as close to a more weather-friendly place, leave it and buy another car or truck. After all, I think we can more than swing something between us. Something that runs. Maybe a rental...If they have rental cars out here."

Totally unsure, Jenny muttered, "I don't know, Fred. I don't know."

"Well," he said, tossing his shotgun in the ranger's vehicle, grabbing Paul's side arm, and then removing the ranger's belt and putting it on. "I can leave you here, in the truck. Someone might find you before you freeze to death. And, if they do, you're gonna have to explain to them who shot the ranger there and why." He indicated with a nod at Paul's dead body lying in the blood-tinged snow, eyes fixed skyward, staring at nothing.

"Shit!" Jenny said, and jumped in the passenger side of the ranger's Suburban, slamming the door.

"Thought so," Fred said, opened the door on the driver's side and got in.

Doug was growing concerned. He hadn't heard from his co-worker and friend, Paul Bates. He'd been trying to get through to him on the radio for a couple of hours now, with no response. When he'd checked in with the ranger's station, Billy Phillips said that Paul had left a few hours ago and was searching for the criminals that had killed Clifford and Bell. But no one had heard from him since about 8 am. This wasn't like Paul. But, Doug realized that sometimes the weather played havoc with the radios. And the weather was bad. He wasn't going to let himself get too worried, yet. But he was getting there. *"Gee!"* he called out for the team to cut a right. They were heading around a bend, taking a trial he often used when exercising his dogs. But today it wasn't for exercise. It was for work. *"Haw!"* Now to the left and around another bend. *"Haw!"* he yelled again. Now they were hitting some open range. Nothing but snow for miles and miles, but far up ahead, mountains in the background, (one could barely see the tops of the lodge and hotel) lay the community of Cantwell and, alongside it, the George Parks Highway, under the snow somewhere. But he wasn't heading to Cantwell. He felt the culprit or culprits were heading south, and south he was going, having his team turn right, now. He headed the team up to approximately where the highway should be and continued on down it. He wasn't sure what he might or might not find. All he could do was search. Besides, he just knew he should be running into Paul Bates anytime soon.

Ranger Billy Phillips was surprised when Joe Screaming Chicken paid him a visit at the station. "What can I do for you, Joe?" he said, offering the old Cherokee Indian who was brushing snow off his shoulders as he closed the front door a cup of black coffee. "Kind of bad weather for just paying a visit." He had seen the old Indian pull up in that old, modified-for-the-weather, multi-colored Ford pickup with a sky-blue hood, yellow-orange right fender, yellow-green left fender, rusty-tan side doors, with a black bed and rear-end that no body could miss, but Joe was an ace mechanic. His old truck could get through just about anything, even where some of the best and newest models of heavy-duty vehicles couldn't.

The Indian's weathered and stoic face said it all. He was here on serious business. "I saw the man that killed Clifford and Bell," he stated flatly in his raspy voice, taking the coffee and sitting down to the side of Billy's desk.

"You did?" Finally some kind of break. "When? Where?"

"I was working on my truck at my garage. Had opened the door for a minute to let some fresh air in and smoke a cigarette, the snow wasn't blowing at that time. I heard shots... four. Two from a small gun. Sounded like a twenty-two. Then two more from a larger gun. I'd say a forty-five. About a minute later, this big man, maybe six-foot-three, a brown beanie on his head, and a light mustache... looked maybe ash blond from where I was, left the store real quick like. He ran around to the back, and the next thing I knew, I saw Clifford's truck peeling out. I should say, trying to peel out. It was swinging back and forth on the slick road. I had the distinct feeling it wasn't Clifford. I was just about to make a beeline across the way when that young Sally Bridges from the lodge down the street ran out and rushed inside. Wasn't but a few seconds later that I heard her scream. I hurried over then. By that time, folks from the hotel were there, too...All eye-balling the dead bodies. But I believe I'm the only one who saw the man run out. Guess I should have called, but I figured Sally had already done that, and I'd get here quicker just getting my truck back in operating condition. And I figured his being a stranger to these parts that he wouldn't get very far very fast, even if the weather should get better. "

"You saw him. That's what counts. I'm glad you got a look at him. Did you see which way he went?"

"Just know he headed south from there." Joe took a generous drink of his coffee and sat the cup down on the wooden arm of his chair. "Would have been here sooner, but had to get the new alternator back in my truck. The other one went out on me. Came as soon as I got it together."

"And I'm glad you did. I'll get the information out to the main office in Anchorage and my rangers in the field immediately, Joe. Thanks...Want another cup?"

"Sure. It's freezing out. I'm in no hurry."

Billy smiled and poured Screaming Chicken a refill.

Shelton cursed under his breath. The plow had warmed up from the engine heat and he'd used it to clear some of the higher drifts out of his path. But he managed, in the interim, to get the heavy-duty pickup off track, and ended up stuck in a frozen heap. "Shit Shinola and save matches!" he bellowed, kicking the door open and stepping out, sinking into three feet of snow. "I'll be a monkey's uncle! Of all the damn luck!" He made his way around the truck twice, analyzing his situation. His left rear tire was buried to the top. He was screwed! *"Shiiiiiiiiit!"* He tore the brown knit beanie off his head and slammed it in the snow. "Dammit! Dammit! Dammit!" And then took in a deep breath and exhaled, making himself look around. Was that smoke he saw off in the distance? He stared for a minute. Yes! It was!

There was a cabin or something about a mile from the road. Smoke rising from the chimney surely meant someone was home. "Bout time I had a break," he grumbled. Hopefully, they won't mind an uninvited guest. And though under ordinary circumstances he wouldn't try to impose on anyone – he wasn't like Fred and Jenny that way – under the present situation, it really didn't matter if they minded or not. He was desperate and he had guns. To his way of thinking, he held the cards. That was just the way it was. He hadn't asked to be abandoned in this no-man's-land.

Lois woke up to Nikki's wet nose in her face. He wanted outside again. She glanced at her watch. Six! "Dammit! Good thing you woke me, Nikki." She tossed her quilt back and ran barefoot into the kitchen to check her stew. It was done except for the potatoes. Nikki was doing a little dance at the back door in the kitchen. "Okay..." she let him out and literally had to push the door closed, the wind was blowing so hard. "Don't get lost out there," she said to the dog. She wasn't worried, though. He loved this weather, and he had such a thick coat of white fur, she figured, he probably never got very cold.

Nikki ran straight on out to one of the two giant silver pines that stood directly behind the house, lifted his leg and did his thing. The wind whipped his face, but there was something in the air, a scent...human, and it wasn't anyone familiar. A low growl rose from his throat. He wasn't a dog to bark when sensing something not quite right, and kept quiet. Instead of doing his usual exploring when let out, he went straight back to the door and scratched, wanting in.

"What the—?" Lois opened the door, surprised to see the dog back so soon. "Damn! It must really be cold out there for you to want back in already."

Nikki didn't express his usual woof at her words; instead he went straight to the living room and plopped down on top of a braided rug that had been placed right in front of the door, something he rarely did.

Thinking his behavior strange, Lois stood in the doorway of the kitchen staring at her dog. "Are you acting as a sentinel now? What's going on, Nikki? This isn't like you?"

Then she had her answer. Suddenly there were two loud knocks at the door. The dog stood, not growling, but baring his teeth. This made her more uneasy, for he was, normally, a friendly dog.

"I'm freezing out here!" a male voice said. "Got my truck stuck back there, went off the road. Saw your smoke. Please! If you can hear me...let me in!"

"What do I do, Nikki?" she said quietly.

The dog stood there, showing his teeth in a somewhat insidious smile.

The man knocked again. "Please! I mean no harm. I am freezing!"

"Guess I can't let him freeze to death." She laid a hand on the dogs head, indicating to him to stay, and then she unlatched the door. A blast of wind gushed snow in ahead of the man as he rushed in.

"Thank you, ma'am," the man with ash-blond hair, mustache, and gray eyes said. He was peeling his wet black gloves off his fingers. "Mind if I dry off?" he asked, swiftly moving over to the mantel and holding his reddened hands in front of the fire. "I really can't tell you how much I appreciate you letting me in, ma'am. I'd surely have frozen to death out there." He turned then, facing her. "My name's Shelton Webb." He extended a hand.

She wiped hers off on her apron and accepted the shake, then dropped her hands back to her sides. She was very uneasy about having a strange man in the cabin with her with Doug not around. And much worse, she wasn't even sure if he would be home that night. There was Nikki, though. She could tell by the look in the dog's keen eyes that he didn't like this man very much. To her knowledge, he'd never tried to bite anyone before – he was one year old when she got him just a little over a year ago – and wasn't sure if he would, being barely out of his puppy hood. Still, knowing the breed, extremely smart and protective, she felt pretty sure that he would, indeed, bite if the situation necessitated it.

"My name's Lois Williams and this is Nikki here." She said, touching the top of her dog's head with her right hand.

"Beautiful dog. A Sammy?"

"Yes. He was a wedding gift from my husband."

"Is your husband around? I see you have a four-door Dodge Ram parked on the side. Looks fully equipped for this climate."

"It is." She didn't want to confess Doug wasn't there, but he wasn't. She feared that if she lied, this stranger would know it was a lie. "Doug's not here right now. He took the dogs out... Likes mushing."

"Oh! A musher," the man said with a pleasant, bordering infectious, smile. "Something I used to think I might wanna do some day. Unfortunately, it hasn't happened, yet." Then, scanning his surroundings, he quickly changed the subject. "Is your husband a cop?"

"A law-enforcement ranger."

"I see," he said and turned back to the fire. "Thought I saw some police-like markings on the side of the Dodge Ram. Couldn't tell for sure, because of the patches of snow on the door."

She had the distinct feeling he was hiding his expression; this didn't help her sense of uneasiness. There was nothing she could do but pray that Doug would return soon, and that her nagging feelings about this stranger would be unfounded. "I have a stew just about ready," she said, making a respectful effort to be hospitable. "I am sure you could use something hot to eat. And I was just about to put some homemade rolls in the oven and make a pot of fresh coffee."

He turned back around, grinning amiably. "Sounds wonderful to me, ma'am. I *am* famished."

"I'll go finish it up then."

"Thanks...You don't mind if I stand here in front of the fireplace for a bit, do you?"

"Don't mind at all. Make yourself comfortable." She gave her dog a signal with her hand down at her side to follow her, something she hadn't exactly trained him to do; she just did it one day, and he had immediately understood. Now, they did it all the time. He wasted no time in following her into the kitchen and plopping down at her feet by the stove.

"Easy!" Doug called to his dogs. There was a truck off the road just up ahead and something else. His heart stuck in his throat as he recognized the brown leather jacket with the fur collar that belonged to his friend, Paul. *"Easy!"* Nook led the dogs up parallel to the truck. *"Whoa!"* Doug stepped off the sled and stuck the snow hook into the ground. He then stood and adjusted his dark sunglasses on his nose. The wind had died down some. Of that he was grateful. But the snow was still heavy. He made his way through the snow and over to the body of his friend lying in supine position, arms out, mouth still gaping open from surprise and eyes staring up at nothing. "Dammit! Dammit all to hell!"

Doug dropped to his knees and closed his friend's eyes. It wasn't going to be easy in telling Nancy, Paul's wife, and Paul's teenage twins, Jodie and Grace, that Paul was dead. Shot from some idiot that obviously wanted the Suburban. He wanted to throw up, but, instead, he stood, kicked at the snow, and then took out his hand-held radio and called in to the station. "BP1... over. Doug reporting in. There's been another murder," then he choked on his words, but finally got the rest out, "It's Paul... He's been shot with a shotgun... He's dead. Over."

There was a slow, "Roger that..." Then a long pause, and then, *"Paul's dead? Over."* Billy could barely control his voice.

"Roger that. Been dead a couple of hours now. Whoever did it took off with his Suburban. Seems the culprit's truck went off the road and got good and stuck in the snow. Over."

"Roger... I'll see if old Screaming Chicken can make it out there to get the truck. Can you bring Paul's body in? Over."

"Roger... I'll strap him to the sled. Over and out."

Jenny had been silent for over an hour, ever since they'd left the dead ranger back in the snow. Fred had definitely noticed his girlfriend's silence, even though he was busy trying to keep the truck on the road. It was snowing again, and heavily. Visibility, once more was terrible. "So," he finally said, "you're not speaking to me anymore?" he asked, looking askance at her briefly. Her mouth was all screwed up and she had an unreadable expression.

"You killed a ranger!" she finally said. "Now we're in real trouble! Guess that's a good enough reason not to feel real talkative."

"What else was I supposed to do?" he snarled.

"I don't know. Seems you could have done something else."

"Dammit! I didn't have a choice. Get that through that thick skull of yours! If we'd gone back, Shelton would have found us for sure! I know him. He's got one hell of a temper. And we both double-crossed him. He would have done his best to get even... Probably kill us."

"He's never killed anyone before."

"Ha! Don't kid yourself, woman. Just because he never did before, doesn't mean he wouldn't ever. And now we've given him good reason. We abandoned him back there. If he told anyone about his truck, it would be found out quickly that it was stolen. Then he'd be connected with swindling that old woman. Nope. We left him without wheels, money and no place to go. We screwed him big time."

She sighed heavily, glanced over at him, and then back to the road, the best she could see it. There were only holes on the windshield where the wipers were working furiously to keep the snow off. "If you ask me, killing that ranger didn't improve our situation. Now, we'll be wanted for murder... *And a law-enforcement ranger at that!*"

Fred's face flushed red. She was pissing him off royal, mainly because he knew she was right. Maybe he had acted hastily, but it was too late to do anything about it now. They just had to get to civilization someplace, abandon the Suburban and get another vehicle. "We'll get through this. You'll see." He reached his hand over and laid it suggestively on her thigh. "And I'll make it up to you. I promise." She smiled, but it wasn't too convincing. He let it go, though. She'd see. They'd be all right. Had to be.

It was late by the time Doug got Paul's body into town and dropped him off at Doctor Pocious' Cold Town Doctor's Clinic (there was no hospital, just one middle-aged doctor who ran everything, including being the local mortician). He went on over to the station and filled out his paperwork. Billy had gone home, but Jasper Cooke was in on the night shift. Jasper was as blond as blond could get without being an albino. And he had ice blue eyes that looked as though he could see right through you. Doug, not normally a man to easily unnerve, often thought he was glad Jasper was on the good side of the law. For Jasper had the most unnerving eyes he'd ever seen. Had Jasper been a criminal, those eyes could easily distract a man from thinking straight. But it was an irony, for Jasper was actually the kindest and gentlest person one could ever meet.

Jasper had made fresh coffee. He gave Doug a cup with a couple of dough-nuts his mom had made (Jasper was unmarried and still lived with his widowed mother, Agnes). Then Doug did his paperwork and headed on home. It would be midnight or later by the time he reached the cabin.

The snow had ceased falling for the moment, though it was still deep, but not too difficult for the dogs to get through. They had been through worse. He wasn't too worried. He'd begin his search again after he had a few hours rest.

Lois had let her dog out around midnight, but stood outside by the door with her coat on and waited until he finished. She didn't want him running off and doing his usual nightly exploring. She considered that maybe he wouldn't, since he was pretty smart. He might sense that he needed to say with her. Still, she still didn't want to take any chances. Doug still wasn't home. She'd furnished Shelton with a blanket and pillow for the sofa, but she didn't want to retire to the bedroom without the dog at her side, not fully trusting the stranger in her house. "Please get you butt home, Doug," she said to the crisp night air. "Please!" About that time, Nikki had finished and ran up to her. "Good dog!" she said and they both went back in.

Shelton appeared to have already fallen asleep, so she quietly made it to her room, hoping not to disturb him. She wanted him asleep. She'd also written a note on a piece of cardboard that was about the size of a sheet of typing paper and tacked to the front door for Doug, so he wouldn't freak out if he walked in and saw a strange man lying on their sofa. She'd tacked the cardboard at the bottom and top. Hopefully the wind wouldn't blow it off, but it did, almost as soon as she closed the door.

Finally, she shut the bedroom door and climbed into bed, but she left the lamp on. Nikki lay down on the floor beside her. She was more than grateful for the dog. If it wasn't for him, she would have been terrified with this stranger in their home.

Shelton had faked being asleep, though he was tired. It was obvious the woman was apprehensive about his being there. He thought it perfectly natural. He had no notions to do anything to her, anyway. She seemed like a really nice person, and she had let him in, though he could tell she didn't really want to. He'd had no place else to go, though. And he was hoping her husband would stay away long enough for him to try and take that truck. That is, if he got the opportunity. Now, he was really beating himself up emotionally for having killed that old man and his wife. He'd just panicked. Panicked! He was actually regretting everything he'd done in the past few months. Swindling that old widow out of her savings had been Jenny's idea, and he'd been tired of working his ass off as a mechanic and never seeming to get anywhere with his life. All he ever wanted was a respectable, well-paying job and to settle down with a beautiful woman and raise a family.

When he met Jenny, he was just floored with her simple beauty. She didn't wear much makeup. Had pretty red hair and fabulous sea green eyes that he could just get lost in. She had a way of getting to him without his even realizing it until she had accomplished what she wanted. "Crap! She was just using me!" he whispered loudly. "Just using me!" He figured the only chance he had now was to go someplace else, change his identity and start all over. Not something he relished doing at forty. Only, how was he going to do all that? He had no job. The truck he had was stolen. *And it was back by the road! Her husband was a law enforcement ranger!* "Dammit all to hell!" he said, not whispering this time. He realized he'd spoken out loud. Shit! He hadn't had much time to think things out. Of course, there was nothing he could do about that damn truck. It was there to stay until the weather either let up or someone could pull it out. But who? He had to get out of there. Had to! He'd known he couldn't stay here long. Now he was feeling real urgent about getting out.

The light from the fireplace lit up the room well enough for him to search around. Where were the keys to that Dodge Ram? He knew it was just getting in deeper. But his ass was screwed when that ranger got home, anyway. He hoped the Dodge could make it through the snow-covered drive to the road, which wasn't much better. He cautiously worked his way around the living room and slipped quietly into the kitchen, eyes peeled for any sign of keys. Then, just when he'd about given up, he saw a set of keys laying on top the refrigerator. He grabbed them. Looked like Dodge keys. Now, if he could just get it started and get out of there before waking her up. He knew it would be damn near impossible, but he had to try. Had to, at least, get it started and drive off before she realized what was going on.

Lois had just fallen asleep when she was awakened by the sound of howling wind coming through the front door. Was Doug home? Damn! She hoped so. She lay there waiting for some time, thinking he was warming up by the fire, anticipating his opening the bedroom door and quietly slipping in, but it didn't happen. Then, all of a sudden, she heard the truck start up. She bolted up in bed. "What the hell?" Nikki was up too and doing a little jig, waiting for her to open the door. She quickly donned her robe and slippers and rushed into the living room with Nikki at her side. By the time she got to the front door she saw the tail lights of their Dodge careening back and forth as it made its way through the snow towards the highway. *"Dammit! He's stolen Doug's truck!"* She stood there with snow pelting her face, staring in disbelief. Then she snapped her head around to the left, for she heard the barking of dogs coming from the north. She recognized Nook's bark – Doug was coming home!

Doug thought he was surely hallucinating when he spotted the red lights of his truck erratically approaching the highway, bearing south, and it was traveling pretty darn fast for the weather conditions. He knew with ever fiber in his being that it wasn't Lois. She rarely drove his truck, said it was too big and she didn't like to handle it, especially in bad weather. Besides, there was no reason for her to be going anywhere at this time of night, especially south. A lump formed in his throat. *Lois! Was she okay?* He yelled, encouraging his dogs on, and Nook picked up the urgency in his master's command and took off with new-found energy. They were at the house in less than five minutes.

Doug was more than relieved to see Lois' standing just inside the cracked open door, waiting for him. After pulling the dogs up and staking them, he ran up to his wife, who had tears in her eyes and was babbling something about how sorry she was for letting the man in. He'd stolen their truck.

"It's okay, babe," he said, holding her and kissing her sweet face. "I'm just glad you're okay." He held her at arms length then. "You *are* okay?"

"Yes! But I'm so sorry!"

"Don't be." He'd found her note and held it up. "It was swirling around in the wind out front."

She took it and crumpled it up in her hand and stuck it in her right hip pocket. She would throw it away later. She quickly filled him in on all that had transpired that evening: how she'd let in this Shelton and, though she'd been apprehensive, he'd seemed okay. She'd fed him and let him bed on the sofa, that she hadn't tried to go to sleep until she thought he was, and then she and Nikki heard the door open. She'd thought it was Doug until she heard their truck start up. But it was this Shelton stealing away.

Then he told her what she didn't want to hear. A pickup he'd found stuck off the side of the road had belonged to old Clifford. It was apparent that this man she had befriended was the one who had murdered Clifford and Bell.

"Oh my God!" Her hands flew to her mouth and her bottom lip quivered.

"At least, he didn't harm you. I thank God for that. Now, I have to go after him. Not only has he stolen my tuck, which is also a law-enforcement vehicle, he stole Clifford's truck and murdered them."

"But how are you gonna catch him? He's in the truck? The dogs are probably tired." She dropped her hands to her sides.

"Honey, the dogs may be a little tired, but they're bred for long hauls in hard weather... Nothing like the Idiatrod to keep them in shape. They're happiest when they're working."

"But what about you?"

"Same goes for me. I have to do this," he said, taking her by the arm and stepping the rest of the way into the cabin and closing the door. "This is *my* job. I don't believe he's the one who killed Paul. Still, I have a hunch that there may be a connection."

"Why do you say that?"

"Just a hunch... A gut feeling."

"And you have reason for thinking this?"

"Yes. I checked with the lodge earlier. Three people, two men and a woman had checked in a few days ago. Monday, I think it was. But none of them checked out. What's more, no one's come back in a couple of days. Their bill was paid in advance though. More than enough. It seemed these people had plenty of cash on hand. What's unusual about it... most people use their bank cards, their Visa, etc. They don't normally go around paying for everything with large amounts of cash."

"Did you get the names of these people?" she asked, following him into the kitchen while he made a quick cup of instant coffee and started packing himself some supplies.

"Yes. There was a Shelton and Jenny Webb, and Fred Masters."

Jenny gasped. "Oh my God! The man that just took off with your truck said his name was Shelton Webb!"

"They must be new at this... giving out their real names. I'm thinking this Jenny is either a girlfriend, wife, or possibly a sister of one of them. And since they'd been showing their money around – why did he rob the hardware? Must be the woman and this other guy took off with all of it, including the truck they were in...Which must be the truck Paul had stopped for – also stolen – and left this Shelton high and dry. And, if I'm correct in all of this, they're all guilty of murder."

"Now, I really don't want you to go, Doug!"

He'd finished packing his supplies and laid the leather satchel on the table. "I've got to go out and water and feed the dogs and put ointment and clean, dry booties on their feet. You can help me with that, if you want?" He said with an inquisitive smile.

"Of course, you know I don't mind helping you."

"But first, I'll let them rest for about an hour after they eat. Then we'll do their feet and then I've got to get going."

"Won't he be long gone by then? Not that I'm in any hurry for you to leave. You know I really don't want you to go at all.

Though I understand you have to," she quickly added, when he got that do-we-have-to-go-over-this-again-look. "But I accept it. Not saying I like it. But I do accept it."

That brought on a soft smile. "He does have a head-start, Lois. But he's green to these parts. Real green, from what I've observed. In fact, I wouldn't doubt but what he's already managed to run the truck off the road. I'll catch up with him, sooner or later."

"Then what? You're one man."

"I take it one step at a time, Lois. This is what I'm trained for. And I'm good at it."

"I know, Doug. It's just scares me. You're practically hunting these killers by yourself."

"Try not to worry. I'm in no hurry to die, Lois. Besides, we haven't had our five kids yet." He smiled again, said he wanted another cup of coffee and turned to make another cup.

She stopped him and said she'd make a fresh pot, so he wouldn't have to drink another cup of instant. He thanked her with a kiss and sat down to the table to rest a minute while the coffee brewed.

"You're driving too fast, Fred," Jenny yelled. "You're gonna get both of us killed."

"Shut your face, woman. We've been stuck four times now, and I've had to dig us out every time. Lot a good you do... helping me."

"The damn snow's heavy. I can't shovel it good."

"Yeah, I noticed. Anyway, at the rate we're going I think we've gone about ten miles. And that's a maybe... stretching it... since we left that dead ranger back there in the snow. We can't afford to stick around here. We've got to make it to Anchorage and get another truck or car. Something that's not so conspicuous." He was staring at her and not looking at what there was on the road. Suddenly, her eyes grew wide and she screamed.

"What the—?" He turned just in time to see a big bull moose standing directly in their path. He tried to brake, but the Suburban went careening off to the right, just missing the moose, and they went sailing off the road a good fifteen feet into a gully filled with snow. After the vehicle came to a rest, snow piled halfway up their windows, and they realized they were still all in one piece and alive, he yelled, *"Dammit all to hell!" Dammit! Dammit! Dammit! We'll never get this thing back on the road now! Never!"*

"You don't need to yell at me!"

"Not yelling at you, nit wit. Just frustrated to the max! Dammit!" he said, beating his fists on the steering wheel.

"Don't call me a nit wit." Jenny mumbled back and huddled in her blanket, insides churning and mind reeling. What were they going to do? They would surely freeze to death now. Teeth chattering, she started to cry. "We're dead," she said. "We're gonna friggin' die out here in this God-forsaken wilderness."

"Not if I can help it!" With that, he tried to open the door, but the snow was piled heavily against it. "Shit!" He tried the ignition, as the Suburban had died when it dropped down into the gully. To Fred's relief, it started back up. "Well, thank God for small favors," he mumbled. He hit the button to let the window down, but the snow began avalanching in. He did his best to scoop it up and toss it back out. "Where's those dang shovels?" he asked, not really talking to Jenny. She was damn near a basket case now. It was more that he was talking to himself. He reached back and found the smaller one. It would do for now. He reached it out through the window and began shoveling snow away from the door the best he could.

Chapter Three

Lois hadn't been able to fall back asleep after Doug and the dogs took off at four am. She was really worried about him, twenty-four hours now without any real rest. And the dogs had to be tired, but as he had let her know on more than one occasion, they were bred tough and could take it. It didn't help her feel any better though, not with all the bad possibilities her mind always seemed to insist in going over. Maybe at times it was a little silly, but this time she knew she had real genuine cause for concern.

She'd made enough fresh coffee for Doug to fill his thermos and there was plenty for another cup or two left over. She filled her mug and sat down in front of the fireplace, and Nikki leapt up beside her on the sofa. She caressed his fine white head with one hand and drank her coffee with the other. He seemed to know she was worried and appeared to be attempting to comfort her, licking her cheek and nuzzling up to her. She laid her arm around him and leaned back against the sofa. "Bull shit!" she said to herself. "Bull shit!"

Doug headed south; the snow had eased up momentarily and he could actually see pretty well. The tracks his Dodge had made were clear and distinct in the fresh snow. It looked as though this Shelton Webb was making good time, in spite of the conditions. But then, his truck was especially equipped for this weather. He was wishing more and more now that he had taken it to begin with. Only, what would that scenario have been by now? Shelton would have still showed up at the cabin. Most likely, there would have been a confrontation, and Lois would have been right in the middle. No. Now that he thought about it, he was glad it hadn't gone down that way; he didn't want his wife endangered in any way.

Doug was the type that believed that all things happened for a reason. One might not always understand or know what that reason was; still there was one behind it. Maybe that was why he had thought of taking the team into town to buy supplies, instead of going in the truck, to prevent an altercation with this man. With that thought, he encouraged the dogs on. They were definitely eager, seeming to sense that something big was going on. He didn't want to push them too hard, though, as they hadn't had much time to rest. He knew that he'd have to find a spot eventually and put up his tent, and let them take a breather, but he just wanted to gain as much ground as he could, while he could. And right now the team had a renewed energy and the snow wasn't falling too hard. Visibility was fairly cooperative. He wanted to take advantage of the situation while it was at hand.

He'd radioed into the station. Billy had just come on duty, and Doug let him know what was going down with him. Billy informed him then that he'd notified the US Park Police and that they had at least one man out searching, too. Also, the entire state was on alert to the situation, but the weather wasn't going to make things any easier. Doug was grateful for any help he could get, for their numbers were few out here in the vast wilderness.

A thought suddenly hit him. Why had he not thought of it before? He had not gassed his truck up, and the last time he had checked only one tank was half full, and the other one was sitting on empty, not something he usually allowed. But he'd been really tired at the time and had just gone inside. As far as he knew, it was the first time ever. Talk about things happening for a reason. He had fully intended to fill both the next time he used it. And, unless this Shelton noticed the gauge, and took the time to fill up from the storage tank beside the house, he would not get real far. There just weren't that many gas stations around these parts. This thought brought on a vague smile. Since the man had left in such as hurry, according to Lois, Doug felt he could almost count on the man having neglected this important little detail. There was a five-gallon red can in the back, but even that needed refilling, as he had given the gas out of it to a stranded motorist the last time he'd had the truck out. His smile grew bigger – Justice was usually served one way or the other, no matter how big or small the transgression.

Joe Screaming Chicken eased his old rebuilt truck up to a stop. A ways to his right was the red Ford pickup abandoned in the snow, the one he'd been told to haul in. Seemed it had been stolen from somebody in Wyoming. He slowly opened his door and stepped down, crunching snow under his boots. It was bright daylight, but wouldn't be for long, as good daylight only lasted a few hours now. He took out his shovel first; no use in trying to pull the truck out until some of the white stuff was removed from around the tires. Just as he stepped off where the road was underneath the snow and ice, he noticed the imprint from where's Paul's body had been and the pink snow just off to his left, right by the deep ridges made by the dead ranger's tire tracks where the murderers had fled the scene. He shook his head. He had really liked Paul, a good man, a family man. Joe never understood why anyone would just kill a man in cold blood like that. He figured it was something he never would understand. He reached the truck and began shoveling. This was going to take a while.

Shelton was trying to sort out all that had happened in the past few hours when he caught sight of an incredibly awesome view of a snow-covered mountain on his right, clouds hanging low, scarfing the bottom, with the peak jutting above the clouds and up into the sky. The road paralleled a drop-off for a good ways, maybe for a half-mile or more. One thing for sure, he didn't want to slide off of that precipice. He slowed down even more, not wanting to take any chances.

About fifty feet away from the road, edging the drop-off, were wooden poles running along every three feet or so. He wondered why anyone even bothered with placing them. Though tall, maybe six feet high, he wondered if the three or four inch round poles would be much good in keeping a fast-moving car or truck from plowing right through and taking flight over that ledge. The thought made him slow down even more. He wondered why he hadn't noticed it before when he, Fred and Jenny had passed by the first time. Maybe he'd been too busy talking. He saw a partially snow-covered green sign with white letters then and could make out the name: *Ryan's Lookout.* Probably a lot of tourists stopped to take in the view during summer vacations.

He still couldn't believe he'd actually managed to get away with the big Dodge before the ranger got home. Now, he planned on taking it as far as he could, figured not too many people would be out looking for him in this weather, and the ranger would be coming by sled, most likely. He'd guffawed at that. There was no way dogs were gonna be catching up with this truck. "No sireeee," he'd said to himself. But then the truck started slowing down. "What the hell?" he'd pressed down on the pedal and it slowed even more. Then his eyes went to the dash. *"Shit!"* Empty!

He sat there for what seemed like an hour, not believing his luck. Why hadn't he looked at the gauge? The damn truck had been parked alongside a gasoline storage tank! It wouldn't have taken him that long to make sure the tanks were full. Come to think if of it, that was probably why the ranger had the truck parked there, to fill up before he went out again. *"Crimanee! Why didn't I pay attention to that?"* But the tanks were probably locked, anyway, to discourage theft. Might not have done him any good to try, but then they might not have been.

What was he to do now? He wasn't even sure how far it was to the nearest town, if there was one between wherever he was and Glenn Highway. There were some villages. He hoped there was one close by. He figured the best he could do would be to get out and start walking and, hopefully, come upon a cabin or village someplace. And, he hoped the ranger wouldn't catch up with him in the meantime.

He sat there for a few minutes more and then finally grabbed as much gear as he could, including snowshoes, taking a blanket that had been rolled up in the back to pull up over himself, if necessary, even though he had donned the ranger's parka, as it was unbelievably cold out. The sun was up, but he knew the days were very short, and he figured he only had a couple more hours of daylight. He grabbed a long-range rifle that he'd seen in the back, adding it to his small arsenal, and then picked up a box of ammo to go with it. Then he started out, thankful that the snow had stopped.

Had been for a while, but he didn't get a few feet and he noticed flakes starting to fall again. "Shit! Just my damn luck!"

Just up ahead was the place where Doug had discovered Paul's body and the stolen truck. Joe Screaming Chicken was there with his old truck and was just getting ready to chain up to the stolen vehicle in order to pull it out of the ravine. Doug pulled his team over and stepped off the sled, ordering his dogs to stay put, not bothering to stake; fully trusting them not to go anywhere. "Need a hand, Joe?"

The old Indian had seen him coming, and wasn't too unhappy about it. "Yeah. Might help. Would you grab the other end of the chain and attach to that trailer hitch on the back?" he asked, indicating with a nod to the stolen truck.

"Will do." Doug picked up the end of the chain with the hook that was beside Joe's pickup and dragged it around. Even with his gloves on, the chain was really cold. "Convenient," he said to Joe, as he secured the hook on the end of the chain in place around the hitch.

"Yeah. It helps when they have a hitch. I'm sure the owner will appreciate us not tearing his truck up."

"Sure they will."

It took a couple of tries, but they finally got the truck pulled out and onto the road. Once on the road, Joe raised the truck up with his pulley, leaving the front end tilted up slightly behind his truck. Finished, Joe thanked Doug, knowing full well it would have taken him twice as long had Doug not come up. But the ranger had noted that it would give his dogs a chance to take a breather. Soon they were both on their separate ways. Joe headed back into town, and Doug searching for his truck, and Clifford's and Bell's murderer.

Fred shot a glance over at Jenny who was sitting and shivering inside the light blue thermo-blanket. "Good thing that was in the truck," he commented, trying to get some semblance of conversation out of her. They'd been sitting there for some time since he shoveled the snow away from the window, not knowing what else to do. Jenny didn't answer. He shrugged and peered out the windshield. "Starting to snow again, woman. We can't just sit here in this Suburban, though it seems fairly warm now. We're eventually gonna freeze to death. Because it's just gonna get colder and colder in here. We have to try and find some shelter, if possible."

A really dark look clouded her face. The prospect of getting out into that freezing wind was not one she relished.

He screwed up his mouth and thought for a moment, and then said, "However..." he craned his head around and his eyes fell on something. "There's a backpack in the seat behind you. Could be it has a small tent inside for emergencies." He nodded towards the seat immediately behind her and indicated for her to look in it.

She did. But there was no tent. "Just some jerky and canned goods, along with an opener," she said, disappointment mounting in her face. She tossed the backpack to the rear of the vehicle.

He sighed deeply. "Probably was a bad idea, anyway. We'd need a fire to keep us from freezing our asses off. But, I thought I saw a cabin a ways down the road behind us. Smoke was coming out of the stack." Still no response. "Okay," he said, exhaling loudly, "have it your way. But I'm not staying here. There's some hip boots in the back. Happens to be two pair. Now ain't that convenient. Just like the good ranger was expecting us to need them." He guffawed at that and opened the door to a cold blast of wind.

That got a stir out of her. "Dammit! Shut the friggin' thing."

"Okay. I will." He stepped out of the Suburban and grabbed the larger of the two pairs of boots out of the back, along with a pair of snowshoes, pulled off one shoe at a time, tossing each in the back, and struggled into the boots. "Nice! Warm! Fur lined. Bet the others are, too." Then he slipped on and fastened the snowshoes.

Silence.

"Okay... Have it your way." He slammed the door to the driver's side, went to the back and took out a larger backpack, one he had searched earlier. It was already packed with survival gear but no tent and started walking away from the Suburban. He didn't get six feet away before she jumped out and started screaming at him to wait for her. "Thought so," he said, sniggering. "Better hurry your ass." He brushed a large flake of white off his nose. It was really coming down now.

She wasted no time in getting out, removing her sneakers and working the boots on and the last pair of snowshoes, and then grabbed the yellow blanket from the back that was rolled up with a belt around it, making it easy to carry. "Might need this," she said, finally forcing a half smile in Fred's direction.

"That's more like it, woman." He turned and began trudging atop the knee-deep snow, very thankful the ranger had unwittingly supplied them with snowshoes. Otherwise, they'd be struggling through the freezing white stuff instead of moving over it.

Daylight was dwindling fast when Doug had the dogs stop off in a cluster of spindly evergreens, pitched a tent and built a fire. Not having any sleep had finally overtaken him, and lack of rest had definitely caught up with the dogs. Soon as he had a quick meal of jerky and now cold coffee from his thermos (he was too tired to make fresh) and had fed the dogs, he snuggled into his sleeping bag and fell instantly to sleep. He'd set his watch to go off in three hours. He couldn't afford to sleep too long, for time could be at the core in catching the murderer, and Shelton Webb, the man who had stolen his truck. He felt pretty sure it was one and the same man. He also decided that when he got up, he'd head back north, towards his place, as he seriously doubted this Shelton had gotten much further than he, even in the Dodge Ram, which was fully equipped for the climate. He'd make a search within a fifty mile perimeter. He felt reasonably sure the culprit had not gotten any further than that.

"Dammit!" Shelton cursed, pulling the fur-lined hood of the parka he'd found in the ranger's vehicle over his head. "Friggin' gonna freeze to death out here in this God-forsaken place." The snow was swirling around him and the wind howling relentlessly. He had three flashlights with him that he'd also requisitioned from the ranger's Dodge Ram. The first one was already showing signs of dimming. "Shit!" He stopped momentarily and did a complete turn around. *Nothing but snow, a bunch of conifers off to his left and more snow!* And it suddenly hit him that he wasn't even sure which direction he was going. Was he heading north? Or was he heading south? Originally, he'd been heading south, or so he thought. But after he'd abandoned the truck, he'd had to stop and rest a couple of times. He'd become a little disoriented and confused the second time, not thinking straight from lack of food and from the long exposure to the severe cold. Had he gone in the wrong direction then? And was there a right direction now? He was so cold he couldn't think.

"Shit! Where in hell am I?"

The wind whipped at him mercilessly and his nose felt like it was going to fall off, even though he had the parka nearly closed across his face. The blasted snow was still swirling down in the biggest flakes he'd ever seen, and it looked like it had no intentions of letting up any time soon. "If I ever catch up with Jenny and Fred after this, they're gonna pay dearly for putting me through this. *They're gonna pay!*" He took in a slow breath and exhaled and then started trekking again, for if he stopped too long, his gut instinct told him that that would be all she wrote, he would be finished. He'd end up a human Popsicle in no time.

Lois warmed up the stew and made herself eat a few bites, but she had little appetite. She'd tried to call Doug over the radio, but hadn't been able to get in touch with him all day. It was probably because the weather was so bad, had gotten much worse since dark, worse than yesterday. Even though he was seasoned to the climate, she still couldn't help worrying that he was hurt somewhere, even lost. Although he had assured her more than once that that would never happen. He knew Alaska like the back of his hand. Though logically she knew he was probably right, it still didn't help the nagging fear she held that something bad was going down this time.

Nikki seemed to sense her uneasiness and came up to her just as she was sitting down to the small table with her bowl of stew and staring at the carrots floating around on the top as though they had some meaning. He whined that high-pitched whine of his and rose up on his hind legs, placing his front paws in her lap, and started licking her face. She put up her hand and gently urged the dog down. "Thanks, Nikki. I know you're concerned for me. But I don't need my face washed at the moment." She indicated with a nod to her bowl, as though he understood. "I'm trying to eat here."

He dropped down but still nuzzled up to her with his fine head. She stroked his head several times. That seemed to satisfy him and he went to lie down by the back door. She made herself finish her stew. All the while, wishing she'd sent more of it along with Doug, but he'd insisted he could carry only so many thermoses. Finished, she set her bowl in the sink and returned to the living room to read.

Nikki jumped up and followed her, placing himself on the red, white and black braided rug at her feet. She picked up her paperback and began reading, hoping she could lose herself in it for a while.

Fred was suddenly aware that Jenny wasn't immediately behind him. He turned, facing into the wind and, with squint eyes against the sting of pelting snow, looked back. He didn't see her at first. "Jenny? Where in hell are you?" No answer. "What the fuck!" He flashed the beam of his light around. Then between sheets of blowing snow he caught sight of her. She'd fallen in the snow and was just lying there. "Dammit all to hell! You can't stop!" He forced himself to brave the chilling wind and made his way back to her. There she lay, curled up in a fetal position shivering and whimpering like a wounded animal. "You realize that if you stay there you *will* die!" he said in no sympathetic tone.

"I can't move anymore," she managed through chattering teeth.

"Hell you can't!" He bent over, grabbed her arm and made her stand. *"We have to keep walking! Have to!"*

"It's no use. We're gonna die anyway."

"Not if I can help it. We've still got all this money," he said, indicating with a nod over his back where he'd stuffed the money in the backpack. "We've stolen a truck... killed a ranger... and stolen his Suburban. You think I'm gonna give up now? I don't think so. And I'm not about to let you go down either. If I end up in the clink, you're going with me! Dying out here would be too easy. Now, let's get moving. I think I see light from a cabin up ahead."

That got her attention. "Where?" she said, suddenly perking up a little. She squint her eyes, looking hard. "Oh! I see it!" she said, a trace of renewed energy in her voice. "I see it!"

"Now, come on! Looks to be about a quarter of a mile from here."

The two of them headed for the promising golden glow up ahead.

It was Nook's wet nose in his face that woke Doug up. He sat up with a start, briskly rubbing his face with the palms of his hands, and glanced at his watch. He'd slept five hours! Not three. And his small fire had gone out. He realized then that he'd been so tired he must not have hit the set button on his watch when he reset the alarm. "Dammit!" He eyed his lead dog. "Thanks, Nook. Just wish you'd woken me sooner. You didn't know, though. He jumped up and quickly rolled up his sleeping bag. "Come on! We've got to get going!" He stuck his head out of the tent opening. At least another three to four inches of snow had fallen since he'd been asleep. For sure, there would be no tracks – not that there were any before – the frozen precipitation had been pretty relentless, even though there had been some breaks here and there. Soon he had his team up and ready. He wasn't exactly sure why, but something in his gut made him veer back due north. For one thing, one of the main reasons he'd taken his dogs, was the weather. And though his truck had been stolen, even with a seasoned, experienced driver in this climate, the weather was too bad in most parts for vehicles to get through very far. He had a feeling that this Shelton had probably gone off the road someplace and was now out trying to find anyplace to get out of the weather, and might even decide to head back to their home, for his and Lois' cabin, was one of very few out in these parts.

The beam from Shelton's second flashlight was now dimming fast. "Crimanee!" It flickered on and off a couple of times and then went out. He stopped in his tracks and stood there for a minute, snow still churning around him, and did his best to look ahead and see if there was anything at all promising in the distance. And just as he was bringing out the third and last flashlight, a large, dark figure suddenly appeared in his field of vision, which wasn't very far in the falling snow. "What the—?" It hit him then that a big bull moose was charging in and the animal didn't look any too happy. "Jeez!" he screeched and did his best to move out of the large animal's path, for he had no time to raise the rifle and take aim, nor time to fish for his semi-automatic that was in his inside coat pocket.

The moose was upon Shelton as he took a desperate dive into the snow, belly down, the moose just missing him. He was afraid to get up, afraid the large animal would charge him again, so he just lay there, face stinging and feeling like it was going to freeze off. Sure enough, he heard snorting, as the moose stood over him, head hung down, sniffing and grunting. *Go away! Please go away!* He thought he was surely doomed. The rifle had gone flying off somewhere. He hoped he'd be able to find it okay, surely there would be an impression in the snow where it fell.

The animal hung around for several minutes and then suddenly snorted one last time and left, leaving Shelton lying in the snow, and actually thanking God (praying was something he hadn't done since he was a small boy of six) that the animal had not killed him. When he felt the moose had gone to a safe distance, he sat up and rubbed his frozen face. "Dammit all to hell! Of all the luck!" Then he reasoned that it could have been much worse. He stood up and felt his pocket for his semi-automatic, still there, and he found the rifle about four feet away, and he commenced walking, traveling in the opposite direction of the moose. He didn't want to cross paths with that beast again. If he did, he hoped he'd have sufficient warning to shoot the bastard next time.

He suddenly realized he didn't have the good flashlight. "Sheeeeit!" He must have dropped it in the snow when the moose charged him. But he didn't want to chance meeting up with the psychotic animal again, so he went on his way in the darkness of night, eyes eventually becoming accustomed to the blackness. He found he could see, not well, but he could see. What little light there was reflected off the snow, which helped. He was thankful for that.

About a third of a mile from where the moose had attempted to run Shelton down, he came across a Suburban abandoned in the snow. He wiped the windows off and saw no one was inside. He made his way around to the driver's side and brushed off the window. It was obvious the vehicle belonged to a law-enforcement ranger. He wondered where the ranger had gone. He tried to open the doors, as he just wanted to get out of the cold wind for a while, but all were frozen shut. Maybe that was a good thing, for he could have frozen to death in the vehicle if he had succeeded in getting in and had gone to sleep. "Shit!" he mumbled to himself and continued on.

Chapter Four

Though it had been dark for a couple of hours, it was still early, barely five-thirty. The main thing Lois didn't like about Alaska, aside from the ofttimes extreme cold, such as now, was the short number of daylight hours. She reminded herself, though, that she was lucky they didn't live further north where it was zero hours of daylight this time of year. That was something she knew she would not be able to handle. Not now. And probably not ever. Her thoughts were interrupted by Nikki scratching and whining at the front door. She'd let him outside only a few minutes prior. Again, as before, he didn't do his usual exploring. And just as she was about to wonder if he had good reason as before, she saw why – two figures struggling across the snow-covered ground, and they were approaching the cabin amazingly fast under the conditions. A man called out, saying they needed help. They'd gotten stuck in the snow up ahead and they needed to get in out of the cold.

More apprehensive than ever, especially since her not-so-fortunate previous experience with a stranger, she really did not want to let them in, but, as they drew closer, she saw one was a woman. It didn't dawn on her at that moment, which she could have kicked herself for later, (but what choice did she have?) that they could be the man and woman that were connected with Shelton.

"Please! Can we please come in?" the woman said, all breathless and sounding fragile and desperate.

"Sure," Lois quickly responded. At the time, she'd thought that they were just a couple of unfortunate, ill-informed, greenhorn, winter vacationers who'd managed to get themselves in a tight spot. She held the door wide for them as they rushed in, bringing in with them a strong blast of wind and snow. They headed straight for the fireplace and stood there, warming their hands, the woman shaking uncontrollably inside her blue blanket. Lois instantly felt sorry for her. I'll make some hot coffee," she said, and rushed straight to her kitchen. She did notice, though, that Nikki stayed parked in the living room, just to the side of the door and held his gaze on the couple. At least, he wasn't showing his teeth the way he had with the other stranger. She hoped that was a good sign. But her hopes of them being safe were soon dashed as she heard the man call the woman Jenny, and then she referred to as him Fred. "Oh my God!" she said under her breath and fell back against the kitchen wall, almost knocking down a small wedding picture of her and Doug. It hit her on the forehead, and she caught it with her hands. They were the other two people Doug had mentioned. But there was nothing she could do now. She had to play along as though she knew nothing.

Having thawed out his hands, Fred removed his coat and helped Jenny with hers, and he hung them on a wooden coat-rack that was just inside the door. Jenny's face was still all pinkish from the prolonged exposure and her red hair was in disarray, but Fred still thought her pretty in spite of what they'd been through. But he didn't like the body language he was picking up from her, the vibes – she was having second thoughts about having left Shelton. "Wish you were with Shelton, don't you?" he said, speaking softly, where the woman in the kitchen couldn't hear.

Jenny gave a firm but slow shake of her head and flatly denied his accusations. "No! No! I'm just exhausted and hungry. Can't even think straight."

"Ya sure?" he questioned, eyes rising as the woman was coming from her kitchen with two brown mugs of steaming coffee. He changed his tone real quick. "Oh! Thank you, Ma'am! Thank you!"

"Yes! Thanks!" Jenny said, brushing a string of red hair back from her face with one hand and taking the mug with the other.

"I'm also warming up some stew I made. There's plenty. I'm thinking you two could use a bite to eat?"

"Sure could, Ma'am." Fred answered, as she turned to walk away.

Jenny rolled her eyes in his direction. "Ma'am?" she said mockingly as Lois returned to the kitchen. "Since when did you call a woman *ma'am*?"

He sniggered. "Since now. She's being kind and considerate. Least we can do is make an effort to be nice back. That is, for now. I have no idea how long we're gonna have to stay here. Don't want to alienate her, yet."

Jenny just twisted her mouth around but didn't respond, keeping her eyes on the mug of hot coffee.

After her guests ate, Lois asked them if they wanted to play a game of Monopoly, since there wasn't a whole lot to do.

They shrugged, shared stares, talked it over for a moment, and then decided what the hell. "Might as well," Fred said.

So, Lois got out the game while they set up the card table in front of the fireplace, and they played for several hours. It was ten-thirty when they decided they'd had enough.

Nikki was standing on his hind legs and doing a little jig at the door, so Lois shrugged on her military green parka that Doug had bought her only a few weeks prior and went out with her dog. She wanted to make absolutely sure he didn't decide to wander off. Chances were that he probably wouldn't, but she still didn't want to take that risk. He was all the protection she had right then. Also, she was still concerned because she hadn't heard from her husband. But she hadn't been able to reach anyone on the radio. The storm was playing havoc with the signals. She hoped it would calm down soon, enough for the radios to work without that ear-shattering static. At least, long enough for her to talk to Doug.

Nikki finished his mission, sniffed along in the snow for a couple of seconds and then ran back up to her. She opened the door and they went inside. Jenny and Fred were on the sofa, sipping coffee.

"Helped ourselves," Fred said, holding up his mug. "Hope you don't mind? It's really mighty good."

"No. Don't mind at all. Glad you like it. Only, if it's okay with you, I think I'll head to my room, but I'll get you some blankets and pillows first."

"That's really kind of you, Lois," Fred said. "Maybe Jenny and I can return the favor some day. If you ever head Oklahoma way." He and Jenny had said they lived in Oklahoma and had come up for a winter honeymoon, and being green to Alaska, had not been prepared.

Lois mentally questioned the fact that they were from Oklahoma, but let it go. She didn't ask any questions, and they offered no information. She brought them their blankets, called Nikki to her bedroom and went in and shut the door. She didn't change into her pajamas though, wanted to be prepared, just in case. She wasn't sure of what, but of whatever might come up.

"Easy!" Doug called to his dogs. *"Easy! Whoa!"* Nook and the rest of the team stopped alongside Doug's Dodge Ram. He figured the thief had run out of gas, for the truck was still where the road should be, though snow was halfway up the tires now. He tried the door and it was frozen shut. But he always carried a small propane torch with him. He dug it out of the pack on the sled and lit it up and after a few seconds of hot flame, the latch unfroze and he was able to open the door. His long range rifle that he kept in the truck was gone. Not a good sign. Not good at all. And he thought it possible that the man could have another gun or two with him, especially if he was the one that shot Clifford and Bell. Their guns had been taken. He scanned the beam of his flashlight around, checking out the area, looked like the man had headed north, straight in the direction of Doug's cabin, even though it was still a long way by foot. He realized the man figured that was the closest he could get to anyplace out of the elements. It was no comforting thought to Doug, though. He seriously doubted that the man would be as nice this time, knowing Lois knew he'd stolen the truck. "Dammit!" Now he had this rising urgency in his blood. He needed to get home! Fast!

Lois was just turning back the covers and climbing into bed when she heard the radio crackle and then Doug's voice. He'd gotten through! She jumped out of bed and snatched up her robe on the way through the door; the two guests sat up in their bed and watched her with great interest as she picked up the microphone. "Roger! Doug! Yes! I'm here! Over!"

"Lois, I think that man, Shelton, is headed back your way. He's run my truck out of gas over here about a hundred feet or so from the overhang at Ryan's Lookout... and the cabin's the closet place to him. *Don't let anyone in!* Over."

As his words cut through the air, she slowly turned around and watched the two visitors get out of bed and slip into their jeans. And she didn't like the looks on their faces. She was starting to feel very uncomfortable.

"Lois? You there? Over."

"Tell him you're okay," Fred said, but it was more like an order. "Tell him we're here."

Lois nodded that she would, but she was having some difficulty in holding it together, but this was not the time to panic. Had to remain calm. Had to!

"Lois?"

"Roger! Yes! I'm here. Just glad to hear from you. I've been trying to call you! Over." Her eyes fixed on the man and woman. Fred was pulling what looked like a .45 semi-automatic out of his backpack. She knew what it was because Doug was no stranger to guns and had several of different calibers he used on his job, and one was a .45.

"Good! You sound... strange, Lois. Is everything all right?"

"Roger. Yes! I have a man and a woman here...Their car went off the road. They've been here for several hours. Over," she said, having difficulty in controlling the anxiety in her voice, though she was desperately trying to remain calm.

Picking up on her fear over the phone, as he knew his wife very well, instantly alarmed Doug, and he didn't want to endanger her anymore than she already was. This man and woman had to be the two that had been with Shelton – His partners in crime. Or, former partners. In either case, things could easily get ugly, and, very quickly. "Roger," Doug replied slowly, keeping his cool the best he could. "Did you give them some of that stew? Over." *Dammit!*

What was he going to do? There was Nikki... but if these people had guns...? Dammit!

"Yes! I did. They liked it," she said, staring at the man and making herself smile amiably. "Over."

"Roger... How's Nikki?" he asked, hoping the dog was close by to her.

She stared at her bedroom door – it was closed! She hadn't closed it! And she realized the woman must have gone over and shut it, for she was now standing by the bedroom door and smiling strangely at Lois, but she suddenly headed for the kitchen. "I'll put some coffee on," she said, and disappeared into the other room.

"Nikki's asleep in our bedroom," Lois said slowly to Doug. But her dog wasn't asleep. She could hear him whining from behind the door. "Over."

"Isn't that him I hear?" Doug asked. "Over."

"No! No!" she lied. "Must be the wind. He's asleep. Over."

There was hesitancy in his voice, but he said, "Roger... Okay. You take it easy and don't let that man in the house. At least, you have someone with you," he said, hoping to appear grateful. "Over."

"Roger... Doug. Just get home. Soon! Over."

"Roger that. Soon as I can. Over and out."

She simply stared at the microphone for a minute, feeling as though she were frozen in time. Was this really real? Was this happening? What was going on? She put the microphone down and looked at the redhead who had returned from the kitchen and was eye-balling her, and fully dressed again. Lois went to go let Nikki out, but the woman rushed up behind her.

"Wouldn't do that, if I were you, Lois."

She tried to ignore her rising fear and replied, "He just needs to go to the bathroom." She turned and looked straight into the woman's gray eyes. "What's going on here?"

"Well, you've been really hospitable, Lois," Jenny answered. "But it seems we have some new development. According to your husband, Shelton is on his way here."

Fred, who'd helped himself to more of the fresh coffee, had a mug in his hand and said, "You see... Jenny and I... Well, we kind of left him back there in Cold Town."

"Oh?" Lois said, trying to walk away from Jenny and heading for the kitchen, but the woman was right on her tail.

"Yeah. He's my husband."

Lois turned and spoke directly to her face, "I see. So he's not real happy with the both of you."

Fred replied for her, "Yep. You're starting to get the picture," He took a sip of his coffee and then held the cup out. "Want some. Mighty good. You look like you could use a cup now, Lois. Look a little pallid."

Lois shook her head. "No. No thanks..."

"Think I'll have some," Jenny said.

Nikki was scratching and whining even louder. Lois turned and headed back for the door.

"I *said* don't let him out!" Jenny stated.

"He needs to go to the bathroom!" Lois insisted, swinging around and realizing she was staring into the barrel of a .45.

"He'll just have to deal with it, Lois."

"It's either that. Or, we'll have to shoot him," Fred warned, sitting down on the sofa. "And he's a mighty fine looking dog. Sure would hate to do that... I like dogs."

"Me too," Jenny said with a fake smile. She lowered the gun and, with her other arm, led Lois back into the living room. "Now you just sit yourself down and rest. Let me and Fred, here, do the worrying."

"Yeah. Everything's under control, Lois," Fred piped in. "We'll just sit here and see who shows up first – Shelton or that ranger husband of yours." He took another sip of his coffee, staring with squint eyes at her over the brim of his cup.

Lois shivered, but it wasn't from the cold. She sat down, but was feeling anything but calm.

The stinging wind had picked up and the snow was pelting Shelton's face mercilessly. "Dammit all to hell!" he muttered and pushed himself onward. "Fuckin' freezing to death here." A strong gust of wind suddenly knocked him off his feet, and that's when he heard or sensed it. He really wasn't sure which, but he just knew. He snapped his head around. The bull mouse had returned – and was charging! This time, Shelton managed to aim his rifle, but just as he fired, another gust caught him and caused him to lunge sideways. And, as a result, he merely nicked the beast across his right shoulder. The animal reared up and let out an awful cry. Shelton knew he was really in for it now. With no time to fire again, he turned and did his best to run in the snowshoes, but he wasn't getting very far very fast. He struggled like a madman, moving as fast as he could, but before he knew it, the animal slammed into him from the side and sent him reeling face down in the snow, knocking his rifle several feet away. He managed to look up at the moose just as it reared up and then came down on the right side of his back, breaking several ribs in the process. He knew he was a goner, but then something got the moose's attention – sounded like some wolves howling off in the distance, and the moose suddenly took flight and disappeared in the darkness.

At first, breathing was excruciating, let alone moving, but Shelton knew he had to. It was his only chance. With a loud cry, he pulled himself up out of the snow and, enduring severe pain, made it over to his rifle. It was then that he saw the orange glow of light from the cabin up ahead. If only he could make it that far. There was a smokehouse off to the side. He'd noticed it when he'd been there previously. If he could get inside, he could hide there for a while; get out of the freezing wind and snow. If only—?"

"What you looking at?" Jenny asked, as Fred stared out a window in the living room. "Thought I heard something. An animal screaming or something. And thought I heard a rifle fire."

"You're just imagining things, Fred," Jenny said, lying down on the sofa where the hideaway bed had now been pushed back in place.

He stepped back from the window. "Not so sure. I did hear something."

"The wind makes all kinds of noises out here," Lois offered, for she had heard it too, not an unfamiliar sound. A rifle had been fired. And the animal screaming sounded just like a moose to her. She'd heard it before, not long after she'd moved up here. Doug had told her then what it was. She could only surmise what had happened, but she figured someone had had an encounter with a moose, and, according to Doug, sometimes they could be really mean. She couldn't help but wondering if the unfortunate person was Shelton. She was sure it wasn't Doug. For one thing, he was with his team. Chances were no moose was going to take on a team of sixteen dogs, unless it was out of its mind. And she hadn't heard any barking, but she had heard a wolf. That she was sure of.

Doug had heard the moose's enraged cry and the rifle firing. It came from the direction he was traveling. Couldn't be too far from the cabin. He kept his eyes peeled for signs of the moose, for he knew it wasn't in any good mood, if it hadn't been killed. It probably wouldn't take on the dogs, but one could never tell about a moose. They had bad tempers. If it was injured at all, it would be more than a bit pissed, and probably any reasoning power (if it was capable of reason?) would be out the door.

Almost there, Shelton gingerly held on to his side with one hand and forced himself onward, though the act of breathing was sheer torture. He was glad the moose had gone off, otherwise he'd be dead meat out there in the snow, and probably wouldn't be found for some time. The dark image of the smokehouse could just be made out now. It was on his side of the cabin, which he was thankful. He desperately needed to stop for a breather before he went on to the cabin, even though it was only another hundred or so feet.

Just as he drew close and felt he was going to make it, he saw the silhouette of a man cross by what he knew to be the kitchen window. He stopped dead in his tracks. Fred! He'd know that profile anywhere! "Well...Well...Well," he muttered to himself. "Wonders never cease!" There was no way he was just going to go up to the door and knock, not with Fred in there. And if there was Fred, there was Jenny. Nope. He wanted to catch them completely and totally off their guard. He changed his direction slightly and finally made it up to the smokehouse and the door. He was glad to see someone had failed to snap the padlock closed. He slipped it out and, after pushing away the snow with his feet, managed to get the door open and slip inside. He tossed the lock aside in the shed, then stuck his hand out the door and did his best to smooth out the snow in front so it wouldn't be so noticeable that the door had been opened. It was still snowing lightly, and the new flakes would soon cover up any traces he might have left.

Shanks of venison hung from the low ceiling, and the building held plenty of smoke. It made him cough, causing more pain, making him think that maybe this wasn't such a good idea after all. But where in hell was he to go? He left the door cracked open slightly and stuck his face to the fresh air, wondering how long he could endure this. "Sheeeeeeit!" He dropped down to his knees on the dirt floor, still facing the opening, and sat back. He had to rest. Had to! At least, the smoke made it warmer inside.

Something in Nikki sensed the intruder, and he whined out even louder, wanting and needing more than ever to get out. Not only did he sense his mistress was in danger, he needed to pee, and now that man had returned. He scratched frantically at the bedroom door.

"Dammit! Can't you shut that damn dog up?" Fred finally snarled, tired of listening to the animal.

"Yeah. If I can let him outside!" Lois snapped.

Fred stared at her dubiously, chewing his jaw for a second. "Okay... But no funny stuff. You make sure he goes straight outside. And just leave him there. I don't trust you or the dog. If he even acts like he's gonna bite, he's dead. Understood?"

She nodded in the affirmative. "Understood."

Jenny escorted Lois to the bedroom. Lois opened the door slowly and grabbed Nikki's red collar, talking to him soothingly, trying to calm him down, and led the dancing and agitated canine to the front door and practically pushed him out, and then she just stood there with the door cracked open, staring out at him as he finally ran out into the snow and hiked his leg at the base of a young conifer, but his dark eyes were on her. She read his face and knew he intended to come back in.

"Shut the damn door!" Fred snarled.

She whip-lashed a dark look at Fred but did as he said. She could only hope her dog would be okay, and she knew Doug was on his way in, but this wasn't really a comforting thought, not much consolation at all. She didn't want her husband in danger, either. These idiots already knew he was a law-enforcement ranger. They had guns. And there was no way she could warn him in advance.

"Sheeeeit!" That damn white dog was out, sniffing around and coming towards the smokehouse. Shelton quickly closed the door, unsure of how long he could stay there in the smoke and no fresh air. And coughing wasn't helping his ribs any. "Crap!"

Nikki was now just outside the door; clawing and woofing, doing his best to pry the door open with his paw. Shelton couldn't stand it any longer; he would surely suffocate in all the heavy smoke or die from the pain of coughing. His lungs and throat stung. And there was always the chance that someone might hear him when he coughed so hard. He opened the door a crack, staring immediately into the dog's black nose. "Go away! Go away!" The dog just woofed and jumped back. Just then, the excited barking of other dogs filled the night. The husband was coming home! Nikki forgot about Shelton and took off in the direction of the incoming sled. "Whew!" Shelton sat back, temporarily relieved.

It was with great apprehension that Doug eased the dogs up in front of his cabin. How ironic, he thought. Everything looked so peaceful, so normal, but he was all too aware that it wasn't. He patted Nikki on the head, greeting the dog enthusiastically, hoping to make himself appear unruffled. He'd made up his mind to take his time, act like everything was okay. Also, he was very aware that Lois would have never left Nikki outside, but here he was. He unhooked the sled-dogs, went around back, noticing the door to the smokehouse was slightly ajar, but did not react – he'd been on the lookout for Shelton, expecting him to be around someplace – grabbed the big sack of dog food that was propped up against the log pile off the back porch, returned to the front, and fed the dogs.

Normally, Lois would have been outside by now. The fact that she wasn't, in itself, was sufficient to let him know something was definitely not right. He moved about, though, taking his time. Though every nerve and sinew in his being was on edge, he had to appear just the opposite. His reactions to what was happening could mean the difference between life and death for his wife and himself. *He had to remain calm! At least, appear so.*

Shelton sat observing with keen interest as the ranger moved about feeding and tenderly caring for his dogs, removing their booties and applying salve, then placing clean booties that he'd taken from his bag on the sled on their feet. The man appeared to be in no hurry. He'd even glanced towards the smokehouse once, but didn't seem to notice anything. Or, was the man just playing it cool? After all, he was a cop of sorts. The only kind they had out here, from what he gathered, except for the park police. He was just glad the dog had seemed to forget about him, but it was probably only a matter of time before all of them would be curious about him. He pulled the door in even closer, barely letting any fresh air in. He hoped that the smoke would eventually cover his scent, and the dogs wouldn't pay him any heed. Oh how he hoped! He started coughing heavily and had to open the door wider, but the wind was howling now and covering the sound of his coughing. The ranger disappeared, apparently he was going inside.

"Get over here, Lois!" Fred said, gesturing in no polite manner, backing away from the front window. "Your ol' man is coming in. Better act normal... or it could get ugly."

Lois jumped up from the sofa where she'd been sitting and praying silently that Doug would not get hurt, and slowly opened the door as her husband approached. "Hi! Honey!" she said, grabbing him as he stepped inside, clasping her arms around his neck, and giving him a big hug, trying to appear cheerful but, at the same time, fighting back tears that wanted to flow, and trembling almost uncontrollably at the same time. She was sure he could feel it.

"Babe," he said, kissing her cheek, but his eyes went straight to Fred and then to Jenny, who had the blue blanket wrapped around her shoulders, though she'd removed her coat. They were standing in front of the hearth, wearing strange, unreadable expressions. Doug nodded, acknowledging them.

"Hello!" Fred said, hands in his hip pockets, but he drew out his right to shake hands with Doug. He had an off-yellow vest on over his red-and-white flannel shirt, and inside the vest, hidden, was his .45.

Jenny smiled and said, "Hello," as the men released hands. She extended hers. "I'm Jennifer... but you can call me Jenny. Everyone else does. And this is Fred."

Doug shook her hand and then dropped his down to his side. "So, got yourselves stuck, did you?" he said, making what he hoped was easy conversation. He nodded in the direction of the kitchen. "Need a cup of *hot* coffee."

"There's a fresh pot," Jenny said, smiling good-naturedly. "Lois just made it. She makes real good coffee."

"That she does," he agreed and went on in the kitchen with Lois at his heels. And the other two weren't too far behind. They didn't want Lois alone with him, if at all possible. This was more than apparent to Doug, but he feigned ignorance to the situation. He smiled down at his wife, but his eyes said it all. He was more than aware of the seriousness of the situation and wasn't a bit happy. "I'm starved! Got anything to eat?"

"Sure do," she replied. "Made sure I set some stew aside for you. In fact, I warmed it up when I heard the dogs coming."

"And it's mighty damn good stew," Fred piped in.

"Real good. Best I've had in a while," Jenny agreed.

As soon as Doug had his stew he sat down to the little table to eat while the others stood around. Lois, who was trying hard not to let the tension get to her, pulled out a chair and sat down beside her husband. "Any luck on finding the person that killed Clifford and Bell?" Her eyes darted off to Fred and Jenny, and then quickly back to Doug.

"I thought maybe it was this Shelton that stopped earlier. I found the truck, as I said before. But I thought he'd be here by now, if he was headed back this way. Obviously, he's not here. Maybe someone picked him up. (He was pretty damn sure Shelton was in the smokehouse, but he wasn't about to give that away.) However, that's really unlikely; the weather's been so bad. There's barely anyone out in this weather that doesn't absolutely have to be."

"That's for sure," Fred said, moving over to the counter and refilling his mug. "Horrible weather. Sure glad your wife was home. We'd surely frozen to death if it weren't for her hospitality."

"Glad to help," Lois said with an affable smile, though she didn't feel like smiling at all. She turned to her husband. "You didn't let the dogs in?"

"Naw," he answered, eyes looking askance where the others couldn't see. "Thought it best to leave them outside... They've been working hard. I was afraid they'd get too hot if I brought them inside now. And Nikki wanted to stay with them. Besides, with all of us here, seventeen dogs could get a little crowded. You know how it is when we let them in. We barely have room to step over them to get around the living room."

"That's very true," she said with an agreeable nod. She had a powerful gut-feeling that wasn't the real reason, though. The dogs were smart. They would have sensed something not right. There could have been complications, and Doug didn't want to endanger the safety of his dogs anymore than he did their own lives.

"And, I need to get my truck back home. I called Joe Screaming Chicken, and he's gonna go out and take some gas to the Dodge, so we can bring it home."

"Now?" she asked, anxiously. "You just got home." There was no way she wanted to be left alone with these two. What was Doug thinking?

"Not now. First thing in the morning. You can go with me on the sled to drive the truck home." He knew she didn't like to drive the big Dodge, but he hoped to get her away from the cabin. "First storm's supposed to be passed by then. It'll still be colder than hell, but no more snow expected for a few hours, anyway."

"I see."

"That's good," Fred said, standing behind Doug. "About time this weather let up," he was chewing his jaw, pondering the situation. "Even if it's only for a short time, it's better than nothing."

"This time of year, this is pretty much par for the course. But the snow's not always so bad. Guess you folks just got lucky," Doug said with an unreadable smile.

"Guess so," Fred replied, bobbing his head slightly, then gave Jenny a nod and escorted her off into the living room.

Lois wanted to say something to her husband, but he held a forefinger up to his lips. "Not now," he whispered. "Later. They're not all of it," he whispered.

"Oh?"

"Later!"

She nodded in the affirmative. She understood.

Chapter Five

The dogs had been lying around, sated from eating and resting, but Nikki had not pulled the sled like the rest, and grew bored after a while and got up and began sniffing around. Strange smells were still in the air. He nosed around the house, sticking his black nose into the snow, sorting out the new and different human scents. Then he came across the smell of the one who had been in his master's smokehouse. The man's scent was not so strong now, as his being in the smoke for so long was beginning to mask, but it was still slightly detectable to the dog's keen sense. He moved about in zigzag pattern until he reached the smokehouse door, which was slightly ajar again. The man was still inside and had fallen asleep.

Snow had piled up about an inch higher since the man had opened it, making it harder to open further, but Nikki managed to wedge his muzzle in and forced the door open wider. He nosed up to the man's face and sniffed.

Suddenly, the man's eyes opened and he bolted upright, cursing under his breath. "Fuckin' dog!" He carefully inched his hand inside his jacket, reaching for his .45, just in case, but a wolf howled in the distance, and Nikki suddenly withdrew his head. Shelton decided it better to close the door than shoot the dog and definitely bring attention to himself. "Dammit all to hell!" He really didn't want to shoot the dog, anyway. Reaching for his gun had been more out of fear of the instability of the situation than anything else. He simply hadn't been using his head.

Nikki ran off for the woods, which began right behind the cabin, seeking out the wolf he'd heard. He was young, very curious and loved to explore. But he had not totally forgotten the man in the shed. He would come back later.

Shelton wasn't sure how long he'd slept, but he touched the button on his watch and it lit up. It was one in the morning. He pushed the door back open a crack. No sign of that nosey dog, it looked as though there was still a light on in the cabin, towards the front. There hadn't been any unusual sounds. He surmised things must still be pretty calm inside. If it weren't for the dogs, he would have tried to slip out and take a peep through one of those windows, but there was no way he could do that with the dogs around. They'd surely notice him.

Inside, Fred and Jenny had gone to bed on the sofa, but they were faking sleep. Doug and Lois had retired to their bedroom, but in spite of the charade amongst the four, things were still tense. All knew that it was probably only a matter of time before something or someone exploded. Doug just hoped he could get his wife out safely first. Before arriving home, he had filled Joe in on the complications at the cabin and told him that he wanted to try and get Lois out of there before all hell broke loose. Joe had grunted in his usual manner and said that he fully understood; that he'd have the truck gassed first thing. And knowing Joe, Doug figured the old Indian had probably already taken care of it, if he'd been able to get out there. And if anyone could, it would be Joe.

Whispering, Lois informed Doug of what had transpired right before his arrival, how they had made her keep Nikki inside for a long time, saying they were going to shoot him, but they finally gave in and allowed her to let him out, but ordered her to leave him there. It was all Doug could do to stifle his inner rage at the thought that they had pulled a gun on his wife and threatened the life of her dog. He'd never wanted to beat any man to a pulp before, but now he did. There was nothing he could do, though, but wait... wait and hope to get her out of there safely in the morning. But he had his doubts. Chances were, they were not going to just let them walk out of there. It would be too easy. Still, deep down, he hoped for what seemed the impossible.

Joe Screaming Chicken hadn't hesitated; the minute he'd gotten off the radio with Doug, he'd filled up two five-gallon gas cans, loaded them up in the back of his old truck and headed out for Doug's Dodge Ram. Once there, he cleared as much snow away from the truck as he could with his front-end plow. He then had to warm the door latch with a torch, as Doug had earlier, and was able to get in a pull the lever to open the gas lids. There were two lids, one on each side of the truck for each tank. The lids over the caps to the gas tanks were frozen too, but he heated up the blade of his pocket knife with the torch and little by little pressed the point of the knife around the lid on the driver's side, until he was able to free it. Once he got the cap off, he poured the ten gallons in, more than enough to get the big Dodge Ram home. Finished, he threw the empty gas cans in the back of his truck, turned around and headed towards Doug's. But he wasn't going to go all the way. He would stop about a half mile before the cabin, walk the rest of the way, and hide in the woods close by. Doug's dogs knew Joe well, as he and Doug often hunted small game together there, the dogs would not pose a problem.

He'd not been able to contact the other rangers, as Doug had asked him to keep trying (Doug hadn't been able to get through either), but Joe had successfully managed to get in contact with Tony Sergeant, the park policeman that had been sent to assist Doug earlier on, but the officer wasn't going to be any help. He'd managed to get his vehicle stuck off the road, and was busy trying to get through to someone from Cantwell to come pull him out. And Joe was much further away, and needed to help Doug.

Jeff Welch had been stranded up further north on another case; some idiot had managed to get himself lost in the storm. As far as Joe knew, Jeff was still on that. Jasper couldn't leave the station, and he'd not been able to get in touch with Billy. The radios still weren't working well in some areas. Joe figured it was pretty much up to him to help Doug.

Hours later, taking his time in the icy conditions, Joe decided to go ahead and drive past the Williams' cabin and then drove on a little further, turned around and drove back about half a mile away, easing off the road just enough to, hopefully, fool anyone who wasn't a native of these parts; make them think that another unfortunate soul, in a tow truck at that, had managed to get themselves stuck. Anyone that really knew Joe would not be worried.

His truck was one of a kind, with all its alterations, different parts from an assortment of vehicles he'd used to rebuild it over the course of several years. And he was constantly making changes to improve its performance over just about any terrain. About the only thing it couldn't do was mountain-climb. And some folks even joked that he'd find away to figure that one out, too. The left front fender was a yellow-orange, and the right, yellow-green. The side doors were a rusty tan, and the bed, top, and rear-end, black. The hood was sky-blue. There was a large plow attached to the front end, and, at the rear, everything he needed for just about any road emergency involving a vehicle, and any others, one could think of.

Joe opened the door and stepped out, crisp snow crunching under his brown leather boots. But he'd be stepping into his snowshoes now. He had his buckskin pouch with a long strap that he pulled over his head, over his buckskin coat, and across his chest. He secured the pouch under his right arm, making it easy to grab whatever he needed. He had a hunting knife stuck in the left side of his belt, and another knife in the pouch, as well as ammo for his guns. He had a Smith & Wesson .38 in a holster on the right side of his belt. He was ready. He stood outside the truck for several minutes. The sun was up but wouldn't be for long. A few hours in the afternoon was all this part of Alaska had this time of year. He wanted to find a good spot to hide before it got too dark. Sleep was something he would worry about when this was over. He took off quickly across the road, towards the woods. He would cross over to the left, behind Doug's cabin, and then find a snug spot in the trees as close as possible, he hoped, without being seen. He'd remove the snowshoes then, as they could get in the way later.

Shelton was tired of breathing the smoke, though he was beginning to grow accustomed to it, eyes weren't watering so much, but his side still smarted something awful. If his ribs weren't broken, they were definitely bruised. He figured someone would be out eventually to check on the fire there in the smokehouse. He'd have to try and hide then – but where? Why hadn't he thought of it before? He chalked it up to being too tired, exhausted, for a better word. In fact, the smoke did seem to be dwindling down quite a bit. He could actually breathe deeper without coughing. He figured it was only a matter of time. He looked around. There were some wooden crates over in the corner, looked like they'd been there for some time, possibly years. There were two stacks. One had three piled up and the other had four. He managed to pull himself up, over, and behind, and then hunkered down behind the four-stack. Yeah. That would work, and, unless whoever came in started looking around, they would probably never notice him. But, the door had been shut and the lock was on it when he arrived. Now the lock was on the floor. Surely they'd notice that minor little detail. Then... maybe they wouldn't. The lock hadn't been secured, it could have been knocked out of place and fallen down from the hard winds of the past day or two. Not likely, but possible.

Sure enough, as though the ranger had read Shelton's mind, he appeared outside and made his way straight for the smokehouse. Fred stepped out with him, apparently to take a smoke, but he kept his eyes on the ranger as he moved towards the building. Shelton hunkered down lower and kept as still as possible, barely breathing, hoping he wouldn't cough.

The ranger hesitated outside the door for a moment, and Shelton just about shit in his pants, afraid the ranger knew he was in there. The door suddenly swung open, seemed the ranger had only stopped long enough to brush some snow away from the door. He then came over and tossed some more wood on the fire and stoked it up just slightly to make sure it kept burning, and then looked around as though puzzled. He seemed to find what he was looking for on the floor by the door, the lock. He stood there, tossing it up and down in his palm, considering the fact that it had been on the floor.

Shelton pretty much held his breath, wondering if the ranger suspected anything, or if he was simply going to pass on finding the lock in the floor, thinking it wasn't important and, hopefully, leave. And Shelton just knew he was going to get locked inside. Only, to his surprise and relief, the man simply tossed it aside by the door where he'd found it and walked out and eased the door shut. Shelton thought that weird, but he was grateful just the same.

Doug was fully aware that there was a man in the smokehouse. He had purposefully not locked it, for the man would surely die from smoke inhalation if he did. He was tempted, though. But he wasn't like that. And, he didn't want a showdown with the others, either. So, he let it go for now. He'd have to take care of one problem at a time.

Later on that evening Doug finally fell asleep, exhausted from the past few days, but Lois never really went soundly to sleep. Every now and then, she'd get up to go to the bathroom and she'd peep over at the sofa where Fred and Jenny appeared to be sleeping, but she had a feeling they weren't really sleeping all that soundly. Doug had his watch set for seven am., but even that wasn't giving him much time to rest. She knew he was anxious about them getting out of there safely. And she was equally anxious, and also worried about Nikki. Normally, he would be inside sleeping with them now. She hoped her dog was off in the woods exploring or hanging out with the other dogs and not in trouble someplace. He was still young and very inquisitive, and had a way of getting into things that an older dog wouldn't dare bother with, like the time he came home with porcupine quills stuck all over his nose. Doug had been home and had taken him over to Joe Screaming Chicken's, who was good at taking care of such things. There wasn't anything she could do about her dog right now, though. She just wanted this to all be over with and things back to the way they had been before, if that was ever going to happen.

Doug didn't have to wait for the alarm on his watch to go off. Instead, he was awakened by the cold hard muzzle of a .45 shoved into his right cheek. His eyes popped open and met his wife's eyes (she was behind Fred), witnessing her tears and horror instantly welling there.

"Easy does it," Fred said. "Easy does it. Now... sit up!"

Doug did as he was told, but his countenance was that of pure, inward rage.

"There's been a slight change of plans. Instead of Lois going along with you to get your truck, I am."

"You've already run one vehicle off the road," Doug retorted as he stood.

"Not my fault. Damn moose got in the way. I won't let it happen again."

"You're the one who killed Paul, aren't you."

"I figured you'd already come to that conclusion. Unfortunate, but it was necessary."

"Shooting a man in the back is *never* necessary!"

"Your opinions don't count here, ranger. Just get your ass dressed... And no damn uniform!" He looked over at Jenny who had entered the room. She now had her gun on Lois. "What does matter here, though, is that you do any and every little thing I tell you to do, right down to the tiniest detail... Or it's goodbye for the both of you. Savvy?"

Doug just glared, face flushed red.

"I asked if you understand... You do understand?"

"Yes! I know what savvy means. I understand."

"You better. Now get dressed. Jenny's already made coffee. She's gonna stay behind here with the wifey while we go fetch that Dodge of yours."

Doug looked over at Jenny. "You sure you can trust him? How do you know he's going to come back for you?"

Jenny's expression revealed instant doubt. Clearly, she wasn't as sure of the character of her choice for a man as she should be.

"Don't let this asshole get you all riled, Jenny. You know I love you."

The tension in her face didn't ease as she blinked her gray eyes, but she said, "Well, I've got the money... half of it, anyway." It was as though she was trying to convince herself.

"Dammit! Woman! What the hell did you mention the money for?"

"Oh! Crap!" Her free hand went to her mouth. "Shit!"

Fred rolled his eyes and shook his head. "And I thought you had brains!"

Doug stood and grabbed his pants off the end of the bed. "What money is she talking about, Fred? You wouldn't be the ones that swindled all the savings from that poor woman back in Wyoming, would you?"

Fred got a twisted smirk on his face. "That would be us." It was almost as though he was proud of it.

Jenny frowned, twisting her mouth around.

"Well, the cat's outta the bag now, woman. Doesn't matter..."

"Where's the other one?"

"What other one?" Fred feigned ignorance.

"The third member of your little party. Shelton wouldn't be his name, would it?"

"How'd you know?" Jenny piped in.

Doug turned his attention to her. "Appears that he didn't get off to too good a start, either. Seems like he's the one that stole my Dodge, after my wife had been good enough to help him out.... Like she did you two! And putting two and two together... I believe he's the one who killed Clifford and his wife, Bell, over at the hardware."

Jenny's jaw dropped. *"He did?* He's never hurt anyone before!"

"Seems he has now," Doug responded.

"See there, woman," Fred said. "I told you he had it in him."

She didn't reply, just stood there, eyes wide, obviously shocked.

"Birds of a feather," Lois said, having gotten her jumbled nerves together somewhat.

"Shut your trap!" Fred snarled.

"You don't tell my wife to shut up!" Doug instantly retorted.

But Fred shoved the gun in Doug's ribs, causing him to wince in pain. "I do! And I did! Now let's get this show on the road!"

Doug stood there staring down at him as though he could kill him just staring, and if the man hadn't been armed, he probably could have. He figured he outweighed him by thirty pounds. He was definitely taller and more muscular.

"Please do as he says," Lois pleaded.

His jaw twitched; stance, rigid.

"Please!" Lois begged.

He finally nodded slowly, considering everything, "Okay, Lois. Okay."

Screaming Chicken had found what he believed to be the best spot, behind the stump of a giant evergreen at the corner of the woods not too far off the road, and surrounded by the big trees on all sides, and just ahead was the clearing where he could get a straight shot at anyone coming out of the cabin, if he deemed shooting anyone necessary. He pulled a brown thermo-blanket out of his pouch and wrapped up in it to aid in maintaining his body heat. It did help considerably that he was among the thick trees, for it was a few degrees warmer there, as the conifers offered some shelter from the elements, mainly the wind. He rested the barrel of his rifle across the stump and sat down, eyes peeled for any movement, and there he sat for hours, until he finally fell asleep. There he spent the night.

He awoke when he realized something was behind him. He snapped his head around and found himself face to face with Nikki, Lois' dog. "Hello there, fella," he said softly to the young dog. "I take it you've been locked out of the house."

Nikki woofed as though he understood.

Joe ruffled the dog's ears and turned his own obsidian eyes back on the cabin. It was still dark, but his vision had become adjusted to the lack of daylight. "At least they didn't kill you. And that... I wouldn't put past them." Something else caught his attention – smoke! Not from the chimney of the smokehouse, but billowing out from the door. *It wasn't shut securely!* Just then, a man stuck the top of his head out briefly, taking in his surroundings, unaware that he was being watched. Then, just as quickly as it opened, the door was closed and the smoke dissipated in a puff. "Now, I know where one of them is, Nikki... I bet you already knew that."

Again the dog answered in his usual manner.

"Guess we'll just sit here and watch for a while. See what this fella is up to. Not a whole lot else we can do, since I have no idea what's going on in that cabin."

Nikki plopped down beside him. It appeared he intended to stay.

"Good dog. Guess you know something's not right at home. Not right at all."

Lois couldn't keep the tears from flowing as Doug and Fred bundled up for their trip. He had the dogs hooked up and ready to go. Fred had gone out with him, watching Doug's every move. But now they were back inside. Lois handed over the buckskin pouch full of jerky, sandwiches and a thermos of hot coffee. There were still some supplies on the sled that Doug pretty much kept ready at all times for emergencies. Doug smiled down at her and touched a tear on her cheek with his forefinger.

"It's going to be okay, Lois."

She swallowed hard and the lump in her throat hurt. "I... I love you," she said softly and tightly grasped his lapels, hugging up to him as though it were for the last time, for she wasn't certain that it wasn't.

"I love you, too, babe," he said and kissed her cheek.

Jenny gave Fred a quick kiss, but their separation wasn't nearly so emotional. She just looked at Lois with a cocked grin. She still had the gun in her belt and was ready to use it, if Lois got out of line, as she had informed Lois earlier on. Fred did tell her to remember Shelton was out there somewhere and could show up at any moment. She replied with some arrogance that she could take care of that gutless wimp.

The men walked out the door with the women behind them, lingering on the porch while they mounted the sled. Doug turned once and waved at Lois, and then he gave the dogs the order to mush, and they were off, Nook charging out in front with his usual enthusiasm.

A tear rolled down Lois' cheek. Normally, seeing her husband work with his dogs was a thrilling and beautiful sight to her, but this time it carried a heaviness about it. She hoped and prayed silently that she would see her husband and his dogs again... and alive.

"It's friggin' cold out here," Jenny said with an irritating whine. "Come on. Let's get our butts back in the house."

Lois only nodded and begrudgingly followed her inside. It was going to be a painfully long wait.

Nikki stood and woofed, tail wagging slightly; he would have loved to have gone with them, but he was bright. He knew he had to stay there. He'd only gone out with the team once and that was when Lois had gone along. It was his place to stay with his mistress. His dark eyes turned in the direction of the cabin where she was. He woofed again, he wanted to go to her, but something in his gut held him back. She did not want him there right now. He wasn't sure why exactly, just that she wanted him to stay outside. He turned his fine head and keen eyes up to Joe, who was observing him more than sympathetically.

"I know you're worried about her, aren't you, Nikki?" Joe stroked the dogs head. "And I hope to see about her soon. But, we have another little problem to deal with first," he said, standing and facing towards the smokehouse. The door was open again and the smoke rolling out. "He's getting more nerve now that Doug and the other guy have gone. What do you wanna bet he's gonna try for the house, Nikki?"

Nikki responded in his usual manner and stood beside Joe, legs dancing slightly, anxious to go.

"Come on! Let's see if we can make our way to the back of the smokehouse without his seeing us."

Doug never had hated leaving Lois so much since they'd been together. She was terrified, not knowing what was going to happen, and he surmised she was afraid of losing him. But he was going to do any and everything within his power to stay alive and get back to her. He didn't want anything to happen to her, either. She was his life. Life without her would now be meaningless, for he had grown to love her more and more each day. She wasn't as crazy about Alaska as he, but she was happy to endure it to be with him. She was not just his wife, she was his best friend.

They'd had too short a time together, not quite two years, yet. And kids... They both wanted kids, but he knew they'd have to move closer to civilization when they started raising a family. But for now, she was happy to be out here with him in God's country, as he called it. He'd heard some refer to the desert in such manner. But to him, Alaska was God's country, and always would be. The regal mountains, the trees, the vastness; the Aurora Borealis when it lavished its beauty upon the night scene, the splendor of it all, was almost overwhelming at times. As far as he was concerned, it was unsurpassed in beauty.

He loved the wild, the wolves howling in the distance at night, the wind singing through the woods, the piercing call of eagles overhead on a clear day as the regal birds hunted for their dinner. Yes! Alaska was his home. Still, he would leave it all for Lois, move to Seattle, if necessary. He was sure he could get a job as a park ranger there, for rangers were scarce just about everywhere, not everyone loved the wild like he. But he'd still keep his cabin and come back for vacations. Lois understood all that he felt. He'd never find another woman to suit him the way she did. He had to stay alive! And he had to get back to her! Had to!

A pack of hungry wolves: a black alpha, two grays and one albino, scrambled across a frozen stream, sniffing along, searching for something to fill their increasingly hungry bellies as the snow flurried around them. It had been several days since they'd eaten, other than a rodent here and there. They were famished and growing weak, but their intense hunger drove them onward. Off in the distance they heard the poignant cry of another wolf, one that was not of their pack. They quickened their pace, seeking out the other wolf. There was always the chance it had found game. In which case, there would be a challenge, a fight for the warm red meat. Anticipating the possibility of a good meal, as they heard the wolf howl again, they broke out into a run across a frozen valley. Woods were just to the far side, where the other wolf was. It mattered not if the wolf was a loner or with a pack, for their hunger far surpassed anything else.

Shelton had observed with great interest as the sled pulled away, dogs breaking out into a run, barking excitedly, and Doug waving back to his wife. He smiled slightly in spite of his painful ribs. Things seemed to definitely be looking up. He figured this was his chance. Jenny was inside with Lois. He knew she had to have a gun, but she didn't know he was there, which gave him an edge. And she'd be all caught up in keeping an eye on Lois, which was convenient for him. He slowly pushed the door open wide, making sure that pooch wasn't around. He hadn't seen him leaving with the sled and team. He cautiously scanned his surroundings. No sign of the dog. He left his rifle inside the smokehouse, and then closing the door all the way and stooping down, he made his way across the fifty or sixty feet to the back of the cabin and to the porch, bracing himself against the wall, and then, slowly looked inside the window to the kitchen. He held his .45 in his right hand, nose of barrel up, alongside his right cheek.

Both women were in the kitchen. Lois wasn't looking any too happy, and Jenny was wearing that satisfied smirk that she'd often worn when around him, when she thought she'd gotten the better of him with one of her snide remarks. He realized now that she never loved him to begin with, had only used him. He seriously doubted that she loved Fred, either. She was just gonna be with whoever she thought was on the winning side, and there her so-called allegiance lay. "Bitch!" he snorted under his breath. "Little redheaded bitch!"

Indian and dog had hesitated at the edge of the property, and in the front of the wooded area; Nikki was a bit antsy and whimpering slightly. "Take it easy, Nikki. We've got to wait for the right moment... Easy."

The dog tossed him an anxious glance, and then turned his black eyes back towards the cabin. He was a good dog, even though he could hardly control himself, he was smart enough to listen to and obey Joe.

Shelton, holding his side with his free hand, inched closer over to the back door and upon reaching it, took another chance and glanced inside. Good! The women were leaving the kitchen and heading for the living room. He slowly reached over and tried the knob. *It wasn't locked!* Evidently the last time Fred had gone out for a smoke, he'd forgotten to lock the door. Shelton waited for a couple of minutes, looking quickly out to the woods behind the cabin and then to the woods to the right. It was starting to get daylight. Now that the men were gone, he felt it really didn't matter. The women out of sight, he slowly and gingerly turned the knob until it clicked, and then he eased the door open slightly and stuck his head in. He heard the women off towards the bedroom. Now was his chance, he quickly slipped inside and closed the door, then hid on the far side of the refrigerator that faced the back door on the far wall. He figured he'd wait a bit and catch the women completely off their guard. Jenny anyway. She was the one with the gun. He wasn't sure how Lois was going to react. After all, he'd stolen her husband's truck. What he didn't see was the white dog and Indian slipping up to the back porch where he'd just come from.

Chapter Six

Doug was confident Fred hadn't paid any heed to Indian' Joe's truck off the side of the road, looking like an abandoned vehicle, and he was sure he hadn't noticed the snowshoe tracks behind the house, leading to the corner of the woods in front. He was pretty positive it wasn't something the greenhorn would be looking for. The tracks were far enough away, as well as the fact that it had still been pretty dark out, that they were hard to notice; barely showing as smudges in the snow from the glow of the kitchen light, but Doug, unlike Fred, had been looking for signs of Joe. He knew the Indian was around somewhere, fully aware Lois was in dire need of help. Just the knowledge that Joe was around someplace, helped; though, it didn't ease all his fears, but he knew Joe would do everything he could to protect Lois and keep her safe. He also knew that Joe was observing Shelton's every move, as well. The Indian had eyes like a hawk and there wasn't much he missed. In fact, Doug credited Joe with most of his own observation skills that the Indian had taught him over their years of friendship.

Shelton could hear the women off in the bedroom, talking, though arguing was more like it. Lois was saying that Jenny and Fred would never get away with what they were doing, that they were just getting in deeper and deeper, and at one point, Jenny hauled off and slapped Lois. And Lois, then furious, hauled off and slapped Jenny right back. By then, Shelton had snaked into the living room and could see the women clearly. Jenny grabbed Lois by the hair at the back of her head and yanked hard, holding the nose of the gun in Lois' cheek. "You don't slap me!" she yelled.

In spite of her predicament, Lois didn't back down. "And *you* don't slap me, bitch!"

Jenny jabbed the gun more into Lois' cheek. "You calling me a bitch?"

"Sounded like it, didn't it?"

Shelton saw his chance. He was upon the women, immediately snatching the gun from Jenny, and now she was the one with a gun to her face. Suddenly, her eyes were saucers of fright. "Where in *hell* did you come from?"

"Been right here... out in the smokehouse for some time now. Watching every move you idiots have made." He nodded in a somewhat respectful manner to Lois but kept talking to Jenny, holding the gun with one hand and his side with the other. "And you certainly don't know how to repay this kind lady's hospitality."

"You stole her husband's truck!" Jenny retorted. "You call that repaying hospitality?"

"That was necessary... for survival. But poking her with a gun," he jabbed the nose of the gun in more, "like this! Well, it just ain't too kind!"

"Fuckin' bastard! Let me go!"

"So, I'm the bastard, now?" He indicated with a nod to Lois that they head for the living room. "If I recall correctly, you and my so-called *best friend* left me high and dry back there in Cold Town. Took all the money. Truck. Everything!"

"It was Fred's idea. Said you'd just pull us down if we kept you with us. That you'd give us away eventually because you don't know when to keep your mouth shut."

"Oh, he did, did he?"

"Yes!"

He shoved her hard, sending her flying backwards to the sofa. "Sit down there while I think this through. And you, kind lady," he said to Lois with a deferential tilt of his head, "I know I don't deserve it, but I sure would appreciate some of that fine coffee you make. Don't suppose you could get me a cup? Been mighty cold out there in that smokehouse. And I got really thirsty. Throat's kind of parched from coughing. All that smoke, you know. Plus a damn moose attacked me earlier. Think I might have broken a rib or two. "

"Oh?" Lois responded, concern in her tone.

"Yep. Damn thing acted plumb crazy. Charged at me for no reason."

"I've heard they can be pretty mean," she stated flatly, as though this were a perfectly normal conversation, but her eyes darted back and forth between Shelton and Jenny. This wasn't the best of circumstances, but it was better than it had been just a few minutes prior, not nearly so tense. Lois just knew she'd have the imprint of that damn gun barrel in her cheek for a long time. It was definitely bruised. "I'd be glad to get you some coffee, Shelton," she said, breaking into a cordial smile as though everything was going to be all right now, even though she knew that was far from the truth. She tossed Jenny a side glance as she headed for the kitchen. And as she walked in, she got a glimpse of Joe's face in the window above the sink, holding a forefinger up to his lips, indicating for her to be silent. She nodded and went about making Shelton his coffee. At last, someone she could trust was there to help, but now she feared for the outcome, for his safety. It seemed that no matter what, there was no way she could feel good about the situation.

Doug, Fred and the team weren't more than a mile from the house when it began to snow again. "Thought you said the storm was over?" Fred quipped.

"The first storm..." He turned his face towards Fred with a smug grin, "Did I forget to tell you there was another... even bigger one on the way?"

"You're shittin' me," he replied.

"Wish I were. Main reason I wanted to get my truck back now. Otherwise, it could be a while."

"Well, that's what we're doing," Fred said, "getting your truck. Only, it won't be you driving it back."

"Yeah?" Doug turned his eyes back to his dogs; they were heading down a rather steep slope. "Better hold on!" he yelled at Fred, just as they started down, the sled veered with great velocity to the right and then back to the left.

"Can't you slow the damn dogs down?" Fred snarled, nearly losing his grip, but managing to stay aboard.

"We're in a hurry. Remember?" Doug gesticulated with his right hand. "Weather!" He indicated towards the blackening sky in the east. The snow clouds were rolling in fast. What had been a completely clear and beautiful sky with a purplish glow was looking very foreboding now.

Doug smiled. It gave him a certain amount of pleasure to be able to get under the man's skin. "Mush!" he encouraged the dogs on. And they took off at even greater speed, now that they had leveled out.

"Dammit!" Fred cursed, doing his best to hang on. He glared at Doug; obviously there was nothing he could do, for he didn't have a clue as to how to drive a team of dogs with a sled. At the moment, he needed the ranger.

Just as Lois sat the tray with three coffees down on the coffee table, there was scratching at the back door. "Nikki!" she could not contain the joy in her voice at hearing her dog. She looked anxiously at Shelton.

"You can let him in," he said.

She rushed to the back door, seeing Joe right behind Nikki, but he wasn't saying a word. He indicated with a strong wave of his hand for her to take the dog on inside. She did, having Nikki go on into the living room with her. She eased down on the sofa beside Jenny and told the dog to come sit at her feet. He immediately obeyed.

"Mighty fine dog!" Shelton remarked over the rim of his cup. He took a sip, and then said, "He paid me a couple of visits while I was in the smokehouse."

"Oh?" was all Lois said.

"Yep. If you ever want to give him up, I wouldn't mind having him."

"I'll keep that in mind," she replied, again speaking as though it were a perfectly normal conversation.

"Oh stop it!" Jenny snapped, shifting her position and taking a cup of coffee from the tray. "You two aren't friends. Quit friggin' acting like you are."

"How would you know?" Shelton sneered. "She certainly beats the hell out of a cheatin' woman like you. She, at least, can cook!"

She glared at him briefly then spurted, "Fuck you!" And looked away, staring off at the fireplace.

He sniggered. Then to Lois, he said, "I am mighty sorry about your husband's truck, Lois. I know you probably won't believe this, but I wasn't going to keep it. Just needed it to get me outta here. I figured you nice folks would get it back. I was just gonna leave it beside the road someplace when I got closer in to Anchorage."

"I see," Lois replied, shaking her head in acknowledgement.

"Shit!" Jenny huffed.

About that time there was a tremendous thud and then a loud clanking, followed by several more heavy thuds on the back porch, sounded like someone hitting bowling balls. All three jumped up, as well as the dog, setting him off to barking.

"Sounds like the wood pile rolling down," Lois suggested.

"That it does," Shelton agreed. "But what caused it?"

"Your guess is as good as mine," she lied, knowing full well Joe was probably responsible.

"I'd better take a look-see just the same," Shelton, angling his .45 barrel ceiling-ward, crept slowly into the kitchen and inched his way cautiously to the back door, Jenny hovering behind. Lois saw her opportunity and quickly slipped away to the front door and unlocked it. She noticed Joe's dark figure to the right side of the building. She then tiptoed back and joined Jenny, who hadn't realized she'd left her side. Shelton now had the back door open and was sticking his head out. Logs were splayed everywhere. "Gonna take a while to stack those back up," he commented.

"Yeah, it will," Lois agreed, knowing that Joe was already in the house and had slipped into her bedroom and was probably in her walk-in closet that Doug had added on especially for her after they were married. She did notice that Nikki had disappeared, too.

He was probably with Joe. She hoped they wouldn't notice the dog's sudden disappearance.

In the back room, Joe put out a hand as the dog stuck his nose in the slight opening of the sliding door. "Not now, Nikki!" he whispered. "Go see Lois."

The dog sniffed, stood there for a minute as though trying to decide what to do.

"Go to Lois," Joe repeated.

Nikki woofed slightly, turned and ran back out of the room.

Joe slid the door almost completely shut, leaving it open only a slight crack. With the bedroom door open, he could see into the living room from where he was. He hoped Nikki would stay with Lois.

Shelton drew his head in and closed the back door. He hadn't seen anything, but he still strongly suspected that the logs didn't tumble down by themselves. They had been stacked pretty securely. The question was – Who else could be out there? Was there another ranger lurking around? Of course, it could have been caused by a raccoon looking for something to eat, or any of a number of small animals. He really didn't think that was the case, though. But his nerves were on full alert.

Doug slowed the dogs down, as they weren't far from the truck now. There was that strange but fascinating, sometimes purple, winter light cast across the snow as the sun was nearing its maximum reach for the day. But the clouds were starting to partially block it. To a newcomer, he was sure the blue-violet radiance made the snow-covered landscape seem like another world, another planet. Still, it was beautiful and strangely serene. Even now, under the pressure of hoping to get back alive and saving his wife, it struck him that he still found it breath-taking. Even Fred was staring at the panorama.

"Kind of pretty, isn't it?"

Fred nodded. "Yep... It is. But this is not any place I'd want to stay permanently. Too cold and too far from everything else."

"Everyone to their own likes and dislikes," Doug stated.

"Yep," Fred agreed. Then he pointed at something in the distance. "What's that up ahead? Looks like a large animal."

Doug saw it then, too. "It's a bull moose. He appears to be wounded... and he's heading straight for us!"

"Why in hell would he do that?"

"Looks pissed. Normally they don't charge in on a team of dogs. Someone must have taken a shot at him. Looks like his shoulder was nicked. One thing you don't want to tangle with is a pissed off moose."

"What do we do?"

"Going to try and evade him," Doug said, and then yelled, "Haw! Mush!" And the dogs veered left, away from where the road was and headed down a slope.

"He's still following us!" Fred yelled, looking back over his shoulder. "Can't we just shoot him?"

"Don't want to kill him unless I just have to," Doug said. "It's also my job to protect the animals here."

But the moose was gaining on them, and Fred stuck the nose of his gun in Doug's side. "Stop the dogs. Now! So I can get a shot."

"I don't want to kill him!" Doug insisted. But the sled hit something rough underneath, causing it to suddenly flip over on its side and the two men went hurtling off into the snow. Doug commanded Nook to stop, shouting, "Woooooooooooooah!" He had landed face down in the snow but pulled up to his knees, staring over a Fred.

The man was on his back, but he quickly sat up, groping around for his gun, which he found just in the nick of time. The moose charged in on him, but Fred fired one shot, hitting the animal straight-on between the eyes and it fell over dead.

"Dammit!" Doug sputtered, cursing under his breath.

"Sorry, ranger. I didn't have much fuckin' choice, now, did I?"

The dogs, greatly excited, were yipping and barking. Doug pulled himself up off the frozen ground and made his way over to his dogs and talked to them soothingly, patting some on their heads, to calm them down, and then he went over to the sled and, with Fred's assistance, turned it right side up. Doug just glared at

Fred, said nothing, and climbed on and indicated with a nod for Fred to do the same. Doug then turned the dogs around and they headed back for the road, his heart heavier than ever that another animal had been killed, and it had probably charged only because it was wounded, though some moose did have nasty attitudes. But who could blame them? Man didn't exactly always treat animals with the respect they deserve.

Shelton stood from the sofa, rubbing his belly and announced he was getting very hungry. Lois stated that the stew was gone but she could make some tuna sandwiches. Doug usually bought the canned fish by the case, so they'd have it all winter. Shelton replied that sounded good, and she went off to the kitchen to make the sandwiches. Nikki was doing his potty dance, so she let him out the back door. She almost felt better with the dog outside, afraid a situation would arise and something would happen, and he'd get shot.

Jenny did her best to avoid Shelton's accusing eyes, shifting several times on the sofa, but it was getting to her. She finally got up and started for the kitchen, but Shelton stood and grabbed her arm.

"Let go of me!"

He shook his head, letting her know that he wasn't going to.

She attempted to yank her arm away, but he held fast. He then slammed her against the wall and kissed her, but she fought him furiously, managing finally to push him off. "Bastard!"

Grabbing his side, he reminded, "I am your husband, you know."

"Not for long!" she sneered and tried to move away, but he put an arm in front of her, still holding her to the wall, but wincing in pain.

Lois stood silently, listening to the commotion in the living room, wondering what was going to happen next. But she didn't have to wait long. The next thing she knew, she heard Shelton yell out and realized Joe had now joined in the struggle. She rushed in. Shelton's gun was lying on the coffee table. She and Jenny eyed it at the same time. Both dove for it. The next thing Lois knew, she was rolling around in the floor in a cat fight with Jenny, pulling hair and swearing like she'd never sworn before. She hit Jenny in the face with her fist, and Jenny clawed at her right cheek.

"Bitch!" Lois yelled.

A loud bang. The gun had gone off. Both women stopped, jerking their heads around to see what had happened. During the men's struggle, Shelton and Joe grabbed for the gun, but Shelton won. The gun had gone off and shot Joe in the side. He fell back against the wall and slipped slowly to the floor.

Lois screamed. "Joe! My God!" She gave Jenny a hard shove, scrambled to her feet and rushed over to him.

"I'm sorry, Lois," he said.

"Sorry? Don't be! Damn!" She swung around glaring at Shelton. "You shot him!"

"The gun just went off, Lois," he said, tired eyes looking truly apologetic.

Lois scanned the area around looking for something to hold over the wound, realizing all the while that Jenny was now standing with Shelton, as though her allegiance had suddenly shifted towards him, and was staring at her with a satisfied smirk.

"I need something... anything!" She jumped up but Jenny swiftly moved over to her and grabbed her arm.

"Where you think you're going?"

"To get a towel!" She stated.

"You're not going anywhere," Jenny informed her.

"Let her get the damn towel, Jenny," Shelton said, flinching from the discomfort in his side. It looked as though it were painful for him to breathe.

"Thank you!" Lois responded, and rushed to the bathroom and grabbed a clean, white hand-towel out of the closet. She hurried back, folded it and applied it to Joe's wound. "Can you hold this?" she asked her friend.

He nodded that he could.

"Well, I'm still hungry," Shelton announced unexpectedly, as though everything was perfectly normal. "Did you get those sandwiches made?"

She looked at him with dismay. "Yes!" she answered, a bit miffed he could still think of food. "But Joe needs medical help now. I need to call someone."

Shelton stood and eyed her for a moment, pondering the situation, and then he shook his head and finally spoke. "Sorry, Lois. I like you. You're a mighty fine lady. Just wish Jenny, here, were like you."

Jenny huffed.

"But she's not. And, as much as I hate the fact that your friend's hurt, I'm afraid I can't let you call anyone. Self-preservation, you know."

"But he could bleed to death!"

"Like I said. Sorry. Besides, it looks like you've got the situation under control now." He then grabbed Jenny's arm and escorted her off to the kitchen.

Lois, eyes full of tears, sat down by Joe. "I'm so sorry."

"It is not your fault, Lois. Don't give up. I'm not dead, yet. And Doug is good at his job. Things could still work out."

"God! I so hope you're right."

The short-lived daylight had succumbed to the approaching hours of night and it was getting close to dark again by the time Doug and Fred reached the truck. The door handle had to be thawed out again. Doug took the propane torch to it and it didn't take long. All the while, Fred stood close by, holding his gun aimed at Doug. He'd told him that one mistake would cost him his life, and probably that of his wife's. At one point, Doug considered turning the torch on Fred, but the man was standing just far enough away to make it difficult. He'd definitely get shot.

Then, as soon as Doug finished with the torch, to make a difficult situation even more difficult, Fred announced to Doug that he wanted him to unhitch the dogs.

"Why?" Doug asked, staring at Fred as though he were crazy, and not intending to give in quickly.

"You're gonna walk home," Fred informed him with a nasty little grin.

"It's too far without the sled. I'll freeze to death before I find shelter."

"Too bad! I can't risk you going back." He motioned with a wave of his gun towards the dogs. *"Now release them!* Or I'm gonna start picking them off one by one."

"You wouldn't!"

"Killed your ranger friend, didn't I? What makes you think I'd stop for a dog?"

"All right," Doug said, screwing up his mouth. "You've made your point." He went over and began releasing the dogs' towlines from their collars. He then unhitched the sled, turned and stared at Fred. "Satisfied?"

"Not yet. Now, we're gonna hook the sled to the back of the truck."

"No!"

Fred wasted no time in swinging around and firing a shot, nicking Nook's right hip. The dog yelped out in pain and fell over on his side.

"Damn you!" Doug hissed and rushed over to tend to his best dog.

"I said hook the sled to the back of the truck! And do it now!"

"Hold on there, Nook," Doug said, gently patting the dog on his head. The dog wagged his tale in the snow in spite of his discomfort. Doug then stood up and proceeded, with Fred's assistance, in pulling the sled over to the back of the Dodge and hooking it up.

"Now," Fred said when they were finished, "I don't have to worry about you reaching the cabin before me." With that, he climbed in the truck, started it up and, giving Doug a big sarcastic grin, managed, after three tries in the deep ridges in the snow, to turn the truck and sled around and head it back in the direction of Doug's cabin.

Doug remained there and chewed his jaw for several minutes, watching the red rear lights of his truck grow dimmer and dimmer.

He could see them in spite of the sled, as the sled was narrower than the truck. Soon, the lights faded entirely, and he finally turned and went back to Nook. It looked as though the bleeding had slowed down. But Doug was more than pissed! He had a large red bandanna in his pocket and tied it around the dog to put pressure on the wound, and then he picked up his dog and, calling out to the rest, began the long trek back home. It was gonna be a long and very cold journey, and the snow was steadily coming down now, but he was determined. The only thing that was in his favor at all was the fact that Fred had allowed him to get his snowshoes out of the sled and put them on. It would have really been near to impossible to get anywhere without them. The snow was deep, reaching the dogs' shoulders in places.

Fred felt smug and proud of himself. There was no way that ranger would make it as far as the cabin in the freezing cold, and the weather was getting worse. But he was becoming accustomed to driving on the snow-covered road, and he was just beginning to think that maybe it wasn't such a big deal after all, when it suddenly hit him that he wasn't sure he was still on the road. "What the hell?" He stopped the truck for a minute, got out and looked around. He could see the tire tracks from where he'd just come. But he couldn't differentiate between the road and the rest of the terrain. "Crap!" He scratched the top of his head. He'd been so busy patting himself on the back that he'd not paid as much attention as he should have. "Sheeeeeit!" He stepped back up into the truck and tried backing it up several hundred yards, doing his best to keep the tires aligned with his previous tracks. He stopped the truck again, got out, and once more surveyed his surroundings. "Bullshit! Where the fuck am I?" He was totally disoriented. And fear slowly began to take over as he realized he didn't have a clue where he was or what direction he was really traveling. "Now get a hold of yourself there," he said. Again he climbed in the truck and began backing up, this time faster, back-end careening back and forth somewhat, weight of sled pulling on it. The rear suddenly veered to the left and he realized it was slipping downhill, sled still attached but buckling at the hitch. *"Sheeeeit!"* He threw the truck in drive and gunned the gas pedal, but it was too late. The truck dropped down even further. And, to his horror, he realized he was going down into a gully or something of the kind. It seemed that his heart was beating ninety-miles-per-hour, but then to his relief, the truck suddenly stopped with a hard jolt.

Fred just sat there for several seconds, waiting to see if it had, indeed, stopped. When he was sure it had, he breathed a loud, "Thank God!" He knew there were numerous streams around, and he wondered if he'd slipped down into one. He hoped not. Even if it was frozen over, the truck was heavy, and with the addition of the sled, even heavier. But he tried to tell himself that it was so damn cold any ice would probably support a tank.

After a bit, he decided to open the door, but snow flakes pelted him as he did. He donned the snowshoes he had in the passenger side of the seat, grabbed a flashlight, and stood by the truck, aiming the beam up to what he now realized was an embankment that the truck had just slid down. "Dammit! I'll never get the truck up that! Never!" He realized he'd even play hell in walking up it. He turned and looked at the truck. It was tilted over to the right, almost lying on its side, sled wedged up against it. "Crap!" It hit him then that he was in the same predicament as the ranger he'd abandoned just a short time before. The irony was that the ranger's chances were now greater than his, for the ranger was trained to survive in this frozen wilderness. *He wasn't!* That revelation hit home to him crisp and clear as he, using the butt of the rifle he'd grabbed from the truck for leverage, began working his way up the steep incline.

The static crackling of the radio startled everyone, for everything had been deadly quiet for some time, no one talking. "Lois! You there? This is BP1. Over!"

Lois jumped up from where she'd been sitting on the floor beside Joe.

"Wait!" Shelton ordered, coming from the kitchen.

"I need to answer it! He'll think it weird, if no one is here."

Shelton sighed heavily but gave her a go-ahead nod.

"Roger. I'm here, Billy. Over."

"Have you heard from Doug? Over."

She paused, wanting so much to tell Billy what was happening. Her eyes went to Shelton who was looking at her darkly and shaking his head in warning. She wasn't sure just how much the ranger knew. "He's out looking for the guy that shot Clifford and Bell, isn't he? Over," she wasn't sure just how much Billy knew.

"Roger that. Okay... Hadn't heard from him. Thought I'd check with you. See if he was there. Obviously, he's not. Over."

"Roger. He's not. Over."

"Roger that. Let me know if you hear from him... Over and out."

"Roger." She put the microphone down, glared at Shelton and went back and rejoined Joe, who was looking pallid. She slid down against the wall and laid an arm around his shoulder.

Shelton just stood there staring at her ambiguously for several seconds and then went back in the kitchen to where Jenny was.

Jasper Cooke knew the second he stepped into the station that something was up. "What is it, Phillips?" he asked, seeing the uncertain frown on his superior's face. He took off his Army-issue parka – he'd been out of the service for a couple of years, but kept his parka and heavy boots – and hung it up on the wooden rack by the front door.

Billy sat his empty coffee mug down on his desk, stood and went to the closet and drew out his own parka, a black one he'd special ordered from a sporting catalogue. "Something is very wrong at Doug's. I finally got through, but Lois said he wasn't home, that he was still out searching for Clifford's murderer. She wasn't her usual warm self. A nervous twang in her voice. And the fact that the radios haven't been working for a good part of the time concerns me. If Doug did need us, he might not be able to get through. And if he's in a tight way someplace, he might not be free to call anyway. Something's wrong. I feel it in my gut." His parka on, he raised the hood up over his head. "Too bad cell phones don't work out here." He sighed, then said, "Gonna take my Silverado and try and make it out to Doug's cabin."

"Roads are still really bad. I barely made it here," Jasper noted. "And Doug's is a lot further out."

"I have to try. Lois is in trouble. I just know it. I've been trying to get through to my wife. But too much static. Got through once, but we couldn't understand one another. So, while you're busy drinking coffee and eating dough-nuts, will you keep trying to call her and tell her I'm gonna be late? Possibly very late."

"No problem, Billy. I'll get right on it."

With a hopeful nod and apprehensive smile, Billy opened the door and stepped out into the freezing, blustering wind.

"Good luck," Jasper called after. But his boss didn't hear. He'd already closed the door.

Chapter Seven

Doug was glad of one thing, the dogs were pretty much staying with him. Now and then one would stray a little ways, hike a leg on a tree or sniff the snow for a rodent underneath, and then return to the rest. Nook had quit bleeding. Doug was thankful for that, but he was worried about infection, needed to get the dog to either Doctor Pocius or Joe as soon as possible. The good doctor and mortician also served as a vet when folks couldn't get in contact with Joe. Joe always had some Indian remedy that usually worked better than a lot of antibiotics.

The air was growing colder, he was sure of it. Of course, it could just be that he'd been in it for so long now that he was starting to lose body heat. That wasn't good, either. And the snowflakes felt more like chips of ice hitting his face instead of soft flakes. Even though he had the hood of his parka pulled up as much as possible with the fur kissing his face, and had it zipped up practically to the tip of his nose, some of the stinging bits still managed to mercilessly pelt him. He thought about Fred and wondered if the man had managed to stay on the road, something he seriously doubted. Even he, at this point, would have great difficulty. The weather was the worst he'd ever seen it. Why now? Why of all times when so much was happening did it have to be at its worst? Or was it that *everything happens for a reason?*

His arms ached something terrible. He stopped long enough to let Nook down and survey his surroundings. He couldn't see very far, but was sure he was headed in the right direction. Just to be sure of his bearings, he pushed the tiny button on his watch that lit up the face with a green glow, and checked the tiny compass that was at the bottom. He was headed north all right. He thought of Lois at home with Jenny. And he was pretty sure Shelton had made his presence known by now... probably Joe, too. "Dammit!" he breathed. "Dammit!"

Nook stood and looked up at him as though to say, "I'm feeling better now! Let's get going."

Doug squatted down and stroked the top of his lead dog's fine head. Nook in turn licked Doug's face. "I know you think you're just fine. And chances are you will be. But we still have to make sure you don't get that wound infected. And it looks like it could use a stitch or two. The only thing good I can think of about the cold right now, is it could possibly slow down any infection trying to set in." He went to pick the dog up, but Nook suddenly whirled around and leaped ahead a few feet, turned and, looking as though he were smiling, barked a couple of short barks. "Okay! Okay, Nook! You're telling me you can make it on your own!" He stared at the dog for several seconds. Nook yipped back at him. Doug smiled and shook his head, "Well, in that case, let's get going!" Nook barked at him again, turned once more, and they continued on their journey, Nook in the lead, just ahead of Doug and the rest of the dogs meandering along, but still managing to keep up.

Shelton had been staring at Jenny fixedly for a long while, and it was obviously starting to get to her. *"Stop that!"* she at last snapped, having had enough.

He twisted his mouth in a cynical smile. "Stop what?" He scooted his chair back from the small table, glanced in the living room where Lois was sitting quietly, squatted down on the floor beside Indian Joe. Neither looked too happy. "Oh well," he mumbled under his breath, and then moved over to the coffee pot and filled his cup with the last of it. "Need to make some more," he said.

"Then make it!" Jenny retorted and turned her face away from him.

"Awe... Does this mean you don't love me anymore?"

She remained mute, jaw set firm.

"Just a little while ago you were making chummy moves in my direction, after that Indian came in on the scene. I take it you were just playing with me again?"

"I don't know what you're talking about," she stated flatly.

"Right!" He went about to rinsing out the pot and making fresh coffee. With the open can of Folgers in his hand, he looked into the living room again. "You folks want more coffee?"

Joe just stared at the man ambiguously, but Lois answered she'd had her fill and then shook her head at the irony in his courtesy.

"Suit yourself," he replied and went back to make the coffee. Finished, he returned to the table and set his eyes on Jenny again.

"I said for you to stop staring at me!" She jumped up and was about to flee to the living room, but he grabbed her and planted her with another kiss. She made every effort she could to push him away, but couldn't work herself free from his grip, for he held her fast. When he finally let her up for air, she spit in his face. And he promptly slapped her hard. Her hand flew to her bruised cheek and she tearfully ran out of the room and into Jenny's bedroom and slammed the door.

Shelton just stood there sniggering scathingly, in spite of the pain in his side. He was hell-bent on making life as miserable as possible for the little two-timing cunt. It made him even madder to think that when he'd first come in she'd had the gall to believe she could pull the wool over his eyes – again! Obviously, she wasn't nearly as bright as he'd given her credit for. At this point, he felt she and Fred very much deserved one another. And she would never, ever, light a candle in comparison to Lois. Too bad he hadn't met that fine lady a long time ago before she'd married Doug, and he had had the misfortune to get caught up with Jenny. He would have turned the world upside down for a woman like her. She was beautiful, smart and most importantly, she was good. "Shit!" he mumbled.

It took some effort, but Fred had made it out of the ravine. Except for the tire tracks left in the snow by the truck, he had no clue as to which way to head. The only directions he was sure of were up and down. Up was out of the question. And he definitely didn't want to go down again. He stared into the gully at the truck that he so desperately needed, but it was fruitless. "Shit... shit... shit!" A hard blast of wind cut across, knocking him over on his knees and palms, leaving him elbow deep in the snow. He sputtered a few more choice words, managed to upright himself, pull the hood of the parka as far over his face as possible and then, with rifle, snowshoes and flashlight in tow, he began his journey, bracing the relentless wind through no-man's-land. All he could do was pray he was pursuing a promising course.

Lois was concerned for Joe. He was pale and beads of sweat had formed on his forehead. She took a tissue from the Kleenex box on the coffee table and dabbed his forehead. He looked kindly to her with his obsidian eyes. It then stuck her as odd that she wasn't sure whose eyes were blacker, Joe's or Nikki's. And why hadn't she noticed it before? Could it be that her senses were more acutely aware and alert under all this stress? Maybe it would be something to ponder, if they ever got out of their situation. The fact that she would notice it now did have a touch of irony in it.

"I will be fine," he said, making an effort to reassure her. "The bleeding has stopped."

"Oh, I so hope you're right." She reached up and laid a cool hand across his forehead. "You're running a fever. That's what I was afraid of... Dammit!" Her eyes went to Shelton then, as he had just entered the living room with a mug of fresh coffee.

"How's he doing?" he said, as though genuinely concerned.

"How do you think? He needs a doctor!"

He placed his mug on the coffee table and sat down on the end of the sofa nearest to them. "I hate that, Lois. I really do. But a man must do what a man must do."

"At the expense of Joe's life?"

"Well, maybe it won't go that far," he said, retrieving his mug and taking a sip. He sat it back down. "We'll just take it one step at a time."

Jenny opened the bedroom door and stepped out, eyes fixed angrily on Shelton.

"Coffee's done!" he said with a big smile, obviously knowing he was just irritating her by being polite.

"Fuck you!" She snapped and plopped down on the far end of the sofa, sitting askance to Shelton.

"Now that ain't polite language for a pretty woman to use," he said, needling her again.

"Fuck you!"

He guffawed and drank down some more coffee, winking at Lois.

Lois just shook her head.

Jenny jumped up again and went into the kitchen. And by the sound from there, she had opened the refrigerator. "Any more of that tuna left?" she said, directing her question to Lois.

"I think there's enough for another sandwich or two," Lois responded. "It's in a blue plastic container." She looked at Joe. "You hungry?"

He shook his head. "No thanks. Not hungry."

"You need to eat to maintain your strength," she insisted.

He turned his head towards her and halfway smiled. "Okay... Lois. If it will make *you* feel better, I'll eat a sandwich."

She jumped up. "Want something to drink?"

"Coffee will be fine."

"Good!" She went to the kitchen.

Shelton eyed Joe thoughtfully and said, "She's really one hell of a nice woman."

"That she is," Joe agreed.

"Just wish she wasn't married... and I hadn't screwed up so bad."

"You can still change things," Joe said.

"No. Too late. I killed that old man and his wife. I really didn't mean to. Hadn't planned on it. I was nervous," he stated, fixing his eyes on Joe's. "The old woman fired at me, and I panicked and shot back... pure gut-reaction. And in the heat of the moment I shot her husband, too. God! I wish I could turn back the clock. I really didn't mean to kill either one of them!"

Joe just stared at him for a moment with his piercing eyes.

"You don't believe me, do you?" Shelton said, leaning forward on the sofa.

"On the contrary, I do believe you."

"What?" Shelton obviously hadn't expected the Indian's response.

"I have been observing you. You're not really mean-hearted. I can tell by the way you act. You're respectful to Lois. You could have killed me right away, as soon as I was wounded, but you didn't. That tells me you're not really a bad person."

It was in his face. Shelton was stunned and speechless for several moments. A hint of tears came to his eyes. "Why... thank you, Joe. That's more than what most people have ever given me credit for... in my entire life."

"If you turn yourself in," Joe said, "I'll testify as to what I've witnessed of your character here. How you've treated Lois and all."

"You'd do that?"

"Yes I would," Joe replied.

Jenny's voice was heard then. Angrily, she entered the living room. "Oh no you don't, Shelton! No you don't! You're *not* gonna pin the wrap on me and Fred!"

Joe regarded her in his matter-of-fact way. "No one said you'd be blamed for the deaths of the old man and woman."

She chewed her mouth around. "Maybe not, but we'll be blamed for the rest."

"Probably."

It was apparent she wasn't sure what to do or think. "I don't know... I don't like it." She looked at Joe. "He killed them. He ought to pay for it."

Joe didn't give her a response, just simply stared back.

"Thanks for your love and support, dear wifey."

"Oh, shut up!" She stomped off back to the kitchen.

Lois passed by her with the tray of coffee and a tuna sandwich for Joe.

Billy had made several attempts to contact Jasper and his persistence finally paid off, and he got through. "Jasper... Billy here. Did you manage to reach my wife? Over."

"Roger that, Billy. She wasn't any too happy. Over."

"Copy that. I assumed as much. But I know Doug needs help. And I've got to find him. Over."

"Roger that, Billy. Over."

"Let me know if you hear from anyone. And I'll do the same here. Over and out."

"Roger... Out."

Billy slowed his vehicle down and came to a full stop, opened the door and stepped out. The snow looked as though it was never going to stop falling. The wipers weren't able to keep up with it. He'd had to stop ever little bit to clean off the windows. He took a scraper to the windshield and then to the back and side windows, got in and continued on, slowly but surely; eyes peeled for any sign of his colleague and friend moving about in the darkness.

Trying to keep his mind off the fact that he most likely was going to freeze to death out in this God-forsaken wilderness, Fred focused on Jenny and his *relationship* with her. It was hitting home that she was fickle as hell. She'd already proven that, the way she'd been acting towards him back at the cabin. There was nothing genuine in her feelings for him (if she were capable of feelings at all, which he doubted), other than possibly loathing. Her affection towards him had simply been an act, an act to get him to turn on Shelton and help assist them in stealing that poor old woman blind.

He knew he was guilty of stabbing his best friend in the back, but he really had fallen in love with the conniving, manipulative little bitch. Or thought he had. He'd just figured she'd had a rough life like he, and needed a strong man to keep her in line.

He'd told himself that Shelton had always been and still was a bit of a softy, just wasn't man enough to hold onto a strong woman like Jenny. Only now, as he trudged across the merciless, frozen terrain, he was beginning to see things much more clearly. She was simply a cold-hearted, selfish bitch that would just as easily cut his throat as Shelton's. He'd never be able to trust her. Never! If he did make it back to the cabin, he was going to have to get rid of her, for he knew she was probably already scheming a way to be rid of him when they got back to civilization, and hoard all the money.

He wasn't about to let that happen, though. Focusing on his burning determination not to let her get away with what he believed to now be the inevitable, taking the money. and possibly leaving him dead someplace, gave him the spiritual fuel he needed to continue on. *"Bitch!"* he snarled into the wind. *"I'm coming! And you'd better watch out!"*

Doug's legs ached from the cold, and he was beginning to feel like a robot, just moving without even thinking, just putting one snowshoe in front of the other, doing his best to maintain a straight course. Some of the dogs had grouped off into small packs and strayed off a ways, but he knew they'd return. They were good dogs. He just hoped they didn't stray too far and run into a pack of wolves somewhere. Nook and a couple of the other dogs stayed with him, though; always faithful, never letting themselves get distracted from their main course. Good dogs... Irreplaceable, in Doug's book. Off in the distance, a wolf howled forlornly, and the way Doug now felt. Nook stopped and hesitated in his tracks for a moment and barked a short response, and then he turned his head and looked back at Doug.

"I know what you're thinking. You're worried about the others. Hopefully, they won't go that far. That wolf sounded a good ways off."

Nook appeared to understand, woofed again, and continued on, taking bounding leaps across the deep snow. Two of the females were immediately behind the lead dog but in front of Doug, whose eyes were stinging from the cold. Unfortunately, there was no way he could cover his eyes to protect them. If the sun was up and shining bright, he could wear his sunglasses, but that wasn't the case. And no way could he stop. Had to keep on moving or freeze to death. He pushed himself onward, doing his best to maintain pace with his dogs, and they seemed to know for sure now which way they were traveling. They had to be heading in the direction of the cabin. They were moving with more certainty in their stride. He felt that was a good sign. But just how far, exactly, they were from the cabin, he couldn't be sure. If only it were daylight and he could see some mountains and make out the tree-lines better, then he could get a much more accurate bearing on his position. But that wasn't the case. He had to rely on his watch-compass and the dogs. Right now, he figured the dogs were his best bet. Their instincts were virtually infallible.

Many hours had passed when Shelton, who had nodded off at the kitchen table, awoke and stood, moving over to the window over the sink. "What do you know – The damn sun is finally coming up. I don't fuckin' believe it. I can see it through a break in the clouds there." He indicated to the horizon.

Lois had come into the kitchen to get Joe some fresh coffee and bring his empty plate back in that had been sitting in the floor since the evening before. She set the plate in the sink and poured the coffee. "Yes. It took me a while to get used to it. This is my second winter here. If I didn't love Doug so much, not sure I would be able to handle it, but I'm getting to where it doesn't bother me quite so much."

"Not love or money could make me want to stay here," Jenny stated. "I've been here long enough now to know that I hate it!" She stood from the table and went to the back door. "Think I'll go out on the porch and get some fresh air. See if the snow looks like it's gonna start in again." She shrugged into her coat and put her blue blanket around her shoulders, opened the door and said, "Your dog's wanting in." She looked back at Shelton. "Should I?"

Shelton eyed Lois. "Think you can keep him under control?"

She nodded that she thought so and replied that he'd been out for hours.

"Okay," he said to Jenny. "Let him in."

Jenny moved aside for Nikki to rush by, flipped the porch light on and stepped on outside. "Brrrrrrr..." She slammed the door.

Lois grabbed a towel and dried her dog off, as he was now wet from melting snow on his fur. She then filled his feed and water bowls and was about to return to the living room where Joe was, but Shelton stopped her, gently taking her by the elbow.

"What?" she asked, looking up, studying him. He really did have somewhat of a kind face. He just didn't impress her as being a cold-blooded killer.

"I just want you to know, Lois. I've been doing a lot of thinking. I really am sorry about all of this. You are too nice a person... and so's your husband. I feel real bad about all that I've put you through."

"But you have no choice, now. Right?"

He sighed and replied, "Yeah. But I feel like a real heel about it."

"I don't know what to say, Shelton. Maybe you should do as Joe said?"

"I don't know. I've been thinking on it. Not sure I can handle years in prison. As a matter of fact... anytime behind bars. I'm sort of claustrophobic."

"Well, if Joe and I both put in some positive words concerning the way you've treated us, it won't change the fact you killed Clifford and Bell... Still, it could make a difference." She eyed him hopefully. "Especially, if you can convince the jury that you reacted out of panic... That you never meant to kill anyone. And, Bell did fire at you first, from what you said. And if that's so, the ballistics investigation may well prove it.

"I sure hope you're right. And Bell did fire first. But I did have a gun on her old man. So, don't know if that's gonna fly."

"You can't lose anything in trying, Shelton."

"I don't know. I'll have to think on it some more."

"All right. You do that. And I'd give it lots of serious thought. I really don't see how things could get any better at this point. But they sure could get a whole lot worse." Leaving him to his thoughts, she returned to the living room. The back door opened and Jenny wasted no time in hurrying inside, swearing like a sailor, mumbling that it was colder than hell could ever possibly dream of out there.

Billy stopped his red, 2007 Silverado and slowly opened the door. There was a large moose lying in the snow just ahead. Looked dead. The sun had finally crested the horizon, peeking its way through a slit in the clouds, causing an eerie but rosy glow across the frozen terrain. This was one of his favorite parts of the day. And it had stopped snowing temporarily.

Though the sun was making itself known, he knew that the storms weren't over. One only had to look around at the heavy, low-lying clouds to see that. It would start up again any minute. He made his way over to the carcass. "Dead between the eyes," he said to himself. He also noticed the other wound on the moose's shoulder. He figured that whoever shot the moose the first time had only succeeded in pissing him off. He figured the animal was charging whoever killed him. An enraged moose was nothing to fool with.

And though the tracks were mostly covered, he could see that there'd been a sled with dogs. Doug! He figured it had to have been Doug, not too many folks would have had their dogs out in the weather they'd been enduring, unless it was a race or something absolutely necessary. But Doug would have done his best not to kill the animal. He loved wildlife. He would have shot the beast only if there'd been no other way. Billy had a gut-feeling someone else had been with Doug.

Something else got his attention then – the howling of wolves. Off in the distance, coming out of a strand of black spruce, was a pack of them, four to be exact, a black one – probably an alpha male – two grays and one white, probably an albino. He figured they had picked up the scent of the moose. They were headed his way. Then he noticed another pack of gray wolves, five in all. The two packs were suddenly running towards each other, challenging for a fight. Figuring there wasn't anything more to do for the moose, he'd just leave nature to her course and he got back in his vehicle and left the wolves to battle over their dinner.

Jenny had secluded herself in the bedroom, leaving Shelton and Lois alone. It was obvious that Shelton really liked Lois, and though she told herself she didn't care, something within her was not only surprised but maybe even a little frightened by it, which disturbed her more than she wanted to admit. She sat on the corner of the foot of the bed, a nice bed with a homemade quilt of red, blue and white squares. The quilt looked fairly new. She ran her hand over the smoothness, had a silky touch. Yet, it was a nice thick piece of work, and she was sure it was plenty warm. Something inside her told her that Lois may have made it. And that possibility just pissed her off royally. In fact, it seemed that damn near everything about that "pioneering" woman seemed to get under her skin. And she knew why, though she hated to admit it to herself. She hated it because Lois was everything she'd never been or would be.

Though she was hard on the outside, and even hard on the inside, there was still part of her that wished she could be the kind of woman Lois was. She figured it had never been in the cards for her. Her mother never wanted her, had pawned her off on Jenny's mother's elderly aunt when Jenny was only four. And though it had been many years ago, Jenny could still remember standing in the doorway of the strange house with a strange woman and crying her heart out as her mother casually walked away and out of her life, getting in the car with a man that wasn't Jenny's father, waving as though she were just off for a few hours, and then she was gone for good. Jenny never saw or heard from her again.

She'd never known her father. He'd bailed when he first learned her mother was pregnant. And the elderly aunt had tried, she supposed, in her own way. At least, she'd fed her and saw to it that she went to school, that is, until Jenny reached high school age. The old woman became too feeble and had to go to a nursing home, and Jenny ran away from the foster home she'd been turned over to. She'd made it on her own then for several years as a hooker. She finally got away from that, but not without getting herself beaten black and blue and being left for dead in an alley and might have died there, but some cop happened along and called an ambulance. That cop, though twenty years her senior, took a liking to her and they married, but it didn't last more than six months. She'd married him out of gratitude, not love. And after a few months of sleeping with a man she could barely stand touching her (she was more than tired of being pawed by men that she didn't want), she just up and left in the middle of the night, after she'd saved up a few hundred bucks and ran off to Wyoming, where she eventually met Shelton and they married after only a few months. He'd paid for her divorce. Fred was his best friend and they were both mechanics at a local garage.

She'd been working down the street for a friend of a rich old woman, Malerie Perkins, who'd been looking for a niece she hadn't seen in years. The old woman figured she didn't have a lot of time left, and she wanted to find her only relative in order to share her wealth with. Jenny had heard this from Malerie Perkins' maid, Mitzie Brown. They often ran into one another in the grocery store and had become friends. That was when Jenny got the instant idea to try and pass herself off as the old woman's long lost niece, immediately putting on an act of amazement by the "sudden" realization in front of her friend. She was the right age and had the right color of hair and eyes. When informed by the excited Mitzie of the good possibility that Jenny was the lost niece, the old woman was overcome with excitement and more than anxious, so the rest was easy.

Once the old woman signed away practically all her wealth to Jenny, expecting her to stay in town and keep her lots of company, Jenny, Shelton and Fred split. And Fred had taken the truck from his ex-wife's new husband while the newlyweds were out of town on their honeymoon, just for the pure thrill of it, getting back at his ex for leaving him.

There had been a time or two when someone had tried to tell Jenny that she could change the direction of her life, and she had tried to an extent. But it seemed that things always went wrong, that the so-called "respectable" life was just not meant for her. Still, it pissed her off that some women had the life she never would. And Lois certainly was one of those women. Lois was like a giant poster facing her, blatantly pointing out all her faults, making her feel like hiding in the back of a dark closet somewhere.

Jenny sat there staring out the window at the frozen terrain. A tear rolled down her cheek, but she angrily wiped it away. "Bitch!" And now her husband had taken a liking to Lois. Even though Jenny had left Shelton for Fred, she still felt the brutal sting of rejection. "Bitch!" she said again, and threw herself down on the bed and just lay there, trying to put all thoughts of all that had happened the past few months out of her mind.

Fred's toes ached, racked with sharp pains, as though someone were stabbing away at them with an ice pick. Though he had on the heavy boots and two pairs of woolen socks, not to mention the boots were fur-lined, somehow, someway, snow must have gotten inside his boots and melted, freezing his toes. And he was pretty much amazed that he was even still moving, but he was.

He had no idea how much further he had to go. The wind continually whipped at him, blowing against him, causing him to walk in a zigzag pattern. If the wind were blowing from the back, it would be easier, help boost him along, get to wherever he was destined a little faster. He hoped it was for the cabin. But there was no way he could be sure.

It wasn't snowing quite so heavily at the moment. He could make out trees and more trees and he was surrounded by mountains. At least, it was daylight again, not that it was helping all that much. He did a left whip-lash when a couple of wolves suddenly started howling not too far off. He didn't see anything. But they were there, somewhere. Maybe even a pack.

He faced forward again and forced himself onward, once more, focusing on Jenny. She'd been so warm and supple the first time they'd made love, but she was also one of the most brazen females he'd ever come across. He guessed that was one of the things he found so exciting about her. She was a challenge. But she could sure turn it on when she wanted something. And she'd really turned it on for weeks when she wanted to take that old woman's fortune, not something Shelton really wanted to do. Yet, there was just something about her that was damn near irresistible, and Shelton had finally given in, even taking Fred in on the job. But

Fred wasn't a "softy" as Jenny often reminded her husband; he'd spent some time in jail for breaking and entering, and he hadn't thought twice about swindling the old hag out of her fortune. But he was thinking twice, now, about his relationship with Jenny. She'd turn on anyone if it suited her whim at the time. He had no doubts that she was now trying to warm back up to Shelton, now being in an insecure situation. Whoever and whatever was handy. That was the way Jenny was. There was no getting around it.

If it wasn't for the fact that he wasn't sure he was going to survive the extreme cold, he would almost be glad for having the time to think about his situation with her. He'd thrown away a pretty good friendship with Shelton for the conniving bitch. And Shelton would never trust him again. That much he was sure of.

The wolves were now howling louder. *"Dammit!"* he breathed. He still had guns, but his fingers were so damn cold, he wasn't sure if he could even bend them. He did his best to accelerate his pace, hoping it really was smoke from a chimney he saw in the far distance and not just remnants from a dark cloud.

Chapter Eight

Lois was glad that Joe's wound had stopped bleeding. She'd put on a clean bandage and was going to get him another cup of coffee, but he said he just wanted to rest for a little, and she assisted him to the sofa where he laid down. She then went into the kitchen where Shelton was making fresh coffee. He offered her a cup in his friendly, good-old-boy, manner and they settled down to the table. Had she not known better, she would have thought him a really nice man as they sat in the kitchen talking about basically everything from things they did in their childhood to how the country had changed over the years, how technology had taken huge leaps in the past decade, with cells phones and digital television. He even had an infectious laugh. Oddly enough, she suddenly realized she actually enjoyed his company. With that sudden realization she became very quiet.

"What is it?" he asked after a few minutes of total silence. "Did I say something wrong?"

She rubbed the bottom of her nose with the back of her hand and raised her eyes back up to his. "No. You didn't say anything. Honestly, it's hard for me to understand how someone who seems so nice as you, could get yourself in such a—"

"Mess," he finished for her. "Yeah..." He leaned back in his chair and stretched his legs out under the table. "I've been kinda wondering that myself, Lois... Especially now, after meeting such a fine lady as you. I realize that maybe what you and Doug have could have happened to me... had I not screwed up my life so damn awful. But now? Well, guess it just ain't gonna happen. Sucks," he said, raising up his cup and taking a sip before sitting it back down.

"You mean meeting me!" Jenny said, suddenly appearing in the kitchen, her face flushed and angry.

He looked up, tired eyes fixed on hers, "You're not all of it. But – yeah! You're some of it. I'd dare say a good deal of it. Had I not listened to you, I wouldn't be wanted for theft and now murder. I'd be back home working my ass off on somebody's Ford or Chevy, making a decent, respectable living. Fred and I might still be best friends... Not that it means much now. I see how loyal he really is. Got you to thank for that. I might not have much, but look what I've got now – Hell to pay! And, yeah, you're a good deal of the blame."

"You bastard!"

He held up a hand. "Ain't finished. I was gonna say – It *is* my fault for falling for your scheming lies. I can only blame myself for that. But it's too late now."

If looks could kill, Shelton would have been dead right then and there. "Damn you!" she said, spinning on her heels and tearing out of the room in a huff.

Shelton shook his head and laughed scathingly after her, stood, then smiling again and gesturing with his mug, asked Lois if she wanted a refill. She declined and said she wanted to go check on Joe. He nodded he understood and refilled his own.

The black alpha wolf, jowl on the right side of his face bleeding from a wound received in the confrontation with the other pack waited patiently for the other three to make it up the hill behind him. They were all still famished, having lost the moose dinner to the challenging pack. He held his nose skyward, nostrils twitching, sniffing the air – the scent of a familiar species was there – dogs. And there were more than one. A fresh gust of wind blew his way and he picked up the scent even stronger. He made a noise in his throat, indicating to the others to follow, and the four headed in the direction of the closest group. His keen sense told him that there were three different packs of dogs. And there was another scent, that of man. Traveling with one man were more dogs. Further in the distance was another man, also heading north, and he was alone, but much further away. It was more in curiosity that the alpha male wanted to check out the dogs, for it wasn't often that they roamed in packs in what he considered his territory. Eager to investigate and still very hungry, they took off, loping across the snow-covered terrain.

The snow had commenced to fall heavier, but Doug thought he could see a faint wisp of dark smoke rising in a curling fashion in the far distance. He hoped it was smoke coming from the chimney of his cabin. Two of the dogs with him seemed distracted. Only Nook remained steadfast, not leaving his side. "Harbor! Shield!" he called out to the two that had been with him and Nook. They came back for a few minutes, but then started wandering off again. It was just too tempting for them. Something definitely had their attention, and he soon realized what – wolves! "Get back here, you two!" he commanded the dogs. Though they were fairly large, they were out-sized by the timber wolves. And, they were outnumbered! "Shit!" he seldom swore, but this was one time he deemed it acceptable. Though he would never shoot an animal unless it was totally necessary, sometimes it was. And he well knew that this could be one of those times, but, unfortunately, thanks to Fred, he didn't have his guns to make a choice. From what he could see, there were four wolves, a big black one was in the lead, and they were heading straight for him, Nook and the two others.

Nook swiftly turned, baring his fangs, hair bristled across his back, standing in guard of his master. And though it wasn't a lot of relief, Harbor and Shield came back and stood ground with Nook. All Doug could do was stand there and hope his dogs didn't get injured too badly, or even worse, killed.

The deep growl in Nook's throat intensified as the wolves came tearing in full speed, and he bolted out to meet the alpha male head-on. The other dogs followed suit, and the battle was on. Snarling and snapping, fur flying. One of the dogs yelped out in pain and went down. It was Harbor, the female. Now it was just two very brave huskies against the big wolves. Doug feverishly scanned his surroundings, looking for something, anything, to use as a weapon. Besides not wanting to lose his dogs, he knew that if they lost, he would be a goner, as well. For in their fighting frenzy they would soon tear him to shreds once the dogs were down. He spotted what appeared to be a broken off branch sticking out of the snow a few feet away. He scurried over. "Yes!" he cried out, as he yanked the four-foot-long stick out of the snow.

Though he knew better than to charge in on a canine clash, it was him and his dogs or the wolves. He mustered up the basic instinctual cry of the soldier heading into battle, screaming at the top of his lungs and swinging the branch with all his might and beating on the head of the gray that had Shield down. The wolf let out a yelp and swiftly turned, but before the wolf could charge in on him, Doug managed another blow to the large canine, and it went down. But Nook was in trouble. Though he was fighting with a fury that even Doug would not have dared dream of, he could see his friend was losing ground quickly. He began swinging the stick again, this time, knocking the black alpha in the side of the head, but it didn't stop him. Shield was up now and joined back in on the fight. It was two dogs to two wolves.

Just as Doug was certain he and the dogs were goners, he heard frantic barking off in the distance. He snapped his head around and saw six of his sled dogs rushing their way back. "Thank God!" he breathed. "Thank God!" For Nook was now down. But the black wolf soon forgot about him and turned to take on the incoming dogs.

Doug stepped back and let the dogs take over completely. He was glad to see Nook get up and immediately return to battle. It wasn't long, though, and the wolves, though they were larger and stronger, were outnumbered and now losing. They gave up the battle and took off. Nook and the rest of the dogs took off after them, snapping at their heels, as though to warn the wolves not to return. Doug called out to them. At first, they kept going, but he finally ripped out a sharp whistle through his teeth, and Nook turned around and the rest followed suit and they came loping back, smiles on their faces and long tongues hanging out, looking very proud of themselves.

"Good dogs!" Doug said, happily. Even Harbor had gotten up. He patted each and every one, hugging them and telling them what great dogs they were. And he meant every word. Tears came to his eyes as Nook, Harbor and Shield enthusiastically licked his face.

He looked skyward, snow pelting his cheeks and forehead, and said, "Thank you, God! Thank you for sparing my dogs and me!" It was then that he heard more barking and saw that the rest of his team had returned. He figured they'd heard the ruckus and were, though a bit late, coming to join in on the battle. Just the same, he was glad to see them. Soon he was surrounded by all sixteen dogs, barking and carrying on excitedly. He let them have their moment of celebration, but then finally got them settled down and they started back on their trek home. Only now there was a certain spring in their stride – a strut of pride.

Billy shut down the engine to the Silverado, slowly opened his door and stepped out, crisp snow crunched under his boots. Doug's truck was down in a gully, and in the back of it was the sled, which told him plenty – Doug was either dead or out in this weather afoot. It had been snowing pretty steadily off and own for the past few hours, covering any footprints or dog tracks that were possibly underneath. He also knew that Doug would never have put that sled in the back of the truck, especially in this weather, for the sled could go places that the truck never could. Someone else had either put it there or made him do it. He straightened the dark sunglasses on his nose. Though snow was still falling, the sun had broken through, causing a blinding glare on the white terrain. It wouldn't last for long, as the sun would set in another hour, but right now, it was harsh on the eyes and made it very difficult to see without dark glasses.

There were still ridges from where the truck had been traveling. It was easy enough to surmise that whoever had been driving it was heading south but lost control of the vehicle. Definitely wasn't Doug doing the driving. Nope. This person had been trying to get away. He took out his hand-radio and was surprised he got through to Jasper who'd stayed on. He filled Jasper in on his findings. In return, Jasper said he'd let Alicia know her husband was okay. He also informed Billy that he hadn't been able to get through to Lois anymore. Either the calls weren't going through or she wasn't answering the phone. None of it looked good. Seemed the picture was growing darker by the minute. Where in hell was Doug? And was he alive? He stepped back up into his truck and gently pulled away, heading back north, moving even slower, sharply scanning his surroundings for any signs of Doug and his dogs.

"Lois! This is Jasper. Do you read me?" the ranger's voice cut clearly over the radio.

Lois eyed Shelton hopefully, but he indicated with a nod again for her not to answer. "Let him think he's just not getting trough."

She breathed out heavily. "Okay, Shelton. But he's not going to keep buying it. Besides, what harm can it do?"

Shelton raised his brow and considered it a moment. "Okay. You can answer, but don't say anything that will give us away."

She nodded that she wouldn't. Eagerly, she answered, "Roger, Jasper. I hear you. Over and out."

"You okay there? Been trying to reach you for some time now. Over."

"Sorry. I was outside for a while. The wood pile rolled down and I was re-stacking it. Took me a while. I didn't hear. Over."

"Roger. Okay! Have you heard from Doug? Over."

She tossed Shelton a quick glance. He shook his head no. "No! Over."

"Roger." Though it was apparent in his voice, Jasper did his best not to sound concerned for the situation. "Okay. Probably just this rough weather, playing havoc with radio transmission. Well, hang in there and let me know soon as you here anything... Anything at all. Over."

It hit her then that Billy should be on duty and not Jasper. "Roger, Jasper. But where's Billy? Over."

"He's out looking for Doug. Just heard from him..." He hesitated, not wanting to tell her that Billy had found the truck with the sled in back, abandoned, knowing full well it would really worry her. "He... He hasn't come across him, yet. Over."

"Oh!" she said, revealing definite disappointment, even though she knew some circumstances of the situation that Jasper didn't.

Still she'd had this feeble hope that Billy had found Doug with or without Fred, and that Doug was on his way home. Only that was obviously not the case. "Roger... Okay... Thanks, Jasper. Over."

"Roger... Over and out."

Shelton came over and stood by her. "Really didn't make you feel any better, now, did it?"

She raised her eyes slightly, shook her head, and flatly stated, "No. It didn't."

"Honestly, Lois. I hope your husband is just fine. And all this works out okay for all of us." He sighed heavily and turned away from her. "Only, I really have no clue how it could." He looked down at Indian Joe who'd just woken up but wasn't looking any too well, shrugged and walked back in the kitchen.

Lois worries switched to Joe. His brow was wet, and his complexion, very pasty. "Joe!" She plopped down in the floor beside the sofa where he was and gingerly reached over and touched his forehead. "Damn! You're burning up!"

Shelton returned to the door of the living room and viewed in. He stood there scratching his chin with his forefinger. "I'm sorry," he said, as she looked at him helplessly.

"Something's got to be done!"

He sucked in air, pondered the situation for a moment and then shook his head. "I can't, Lois. I can't do anything for him."

"You can let me call someone!" She said, now standing. "Please!"

"And even if you do, and you do get through, you think they're gonna be able to make it out here?" He waved his mug in the air, indicating for her to look out the window. "Even with the best transportation that can be gotten, anyone's gonna play hell in getting out here anytime soon."

"I will be okay," Joe said, trying to assure her that he would be. "I've been worse."

"I don't see how," she said, knowing what he was doing.

"The bullet needs to come out," Shelton said.

"Exactly!" Lois stated. "That's why we need to get him medical attention soon as possible!"

"Yes," Joe agreed. "It does need to come out, Lois." He looked up at her.

His expression instantly made her uneasy. "What?" she asked.

"I could walk you through it."

She stared at him for a few seconds and then said, "Oh my God! You want me to cut it out?" She shook just at the notion of it. "Shit! I can't even stand the sight of my own blood... let alone... someone else's."

"I can do it!" Shelton said, sitting his cup on the coffee table.

"You can?" Lois shot him an inquisitive look.

"You said you could lead her through it, didn't you, Joe?"

The Indian answered with a nod of his head that that was correct.

"Well, you can lead me through it just as well. That is, if you're willing to trust me?" He looked at the Indian with a purity of assurance in his intentions.

"If you say you can do it... Then let's do it," Joe said. "Lois, start boiling some water. And gather up plenty of clean towels... preferably white."

She stood there momentarily staring at the both of them as though they were completely crazy. But Joe finally stated that he really needed her to do this, and he was counting on her, and she finally said that she would and hurried out to the kitchen to put the pan of water on to boil.

Jenny had come out of the bedroom and had been standing just inside the living room taking everything in. She followed Shelton into the bathroom where he was scrubbing his hands in hot soapy water. "You're really gonna take that bullet out?"

He turned his head her way. "You have a problem with that?"

"Just surprised me... Is all."

"What? That I care if the man lives or dies?"

She just eyed him mutely for several seconds then shrugged. "Do what the fuck you want. Doesn't matter to me."

He snorted at her lack of compassion and returned to washing his hands.

Fred, shivering hard inside his parka, and realizing his eyebrows and the tip of his nose were growing icicles, somehow drew up the courage to keep placing one foot in front of the other. It was a mechanical thing now, as though his legs were attached to someone or something else. Why, he didn't even feel them anymore. And it didn't help that the short hours of sunlight were speedily dwindling. It would be dark again. And very soon. "I'm already dead," he mumbled to himself. But he was stubborn and kept going. "Already dead. Body's just too stupid to know it."

The black alpha male sensed the other male human was not too far in the distance. Still excited and irritated from the encounter with the first man and his dogs, he was still bristling for something more, not happy having lost either one of their previous battles. With deep guttural sounds from within his throat, he let the others know he wanted to pursue the man-scent. They took off bounding the best they could in the deep snow.

Fred wasn't exactly sure what it was, but something made him turn around. *"Holy mother of God!"* he cried aloud, for right in front of him were four wolves, and it was beyond any doubt that they meant business. Their lips were curled and they were snarling viciously. *"Oh... sweet Jesus!"* he susurrated as he, with trembling, freezing hands, lowered the barrel of the rifle, making an effort to take aim. He did his best to home in on the big fellow in front, which definitely wasn't playing around. Then, just as the black wolf leapt high in the air, Fred managed to fire off a shot, just nicking the wolf across the bottom of his left jaw, but the kick from the blast was sufficient enough to throw Fred in his greatly weakened condition aside to the ground. Somehow, though, he managed to maintain grasp of his rifle.

The black one down momentarily, Fred fired again at a gray that was now almost on top of him (while the albino bit through his boot and tore at his ankle) hitting it squarely in its forehead, killing it instantly. It fell over. By then, the other gray was on top, attempting a go for Fred's throat. He screamed out like a terrified child as the wolf clamped down onto his jaw, but he fought with everything he had to finally grab the loose skin on the wolf's neck long enough to throw him aside and clobber its head with the butt of his rifle, stunning it, only to find himself staring into the ice blue eyes of the white one. He still held a good grip on the middle of the rifle, and there was sufficient space between him and the wolf that he hammered the butt of the rifle down hard, claiming the animal's skull in such an angle that it killed him instantly. Left were the black male and the one last gray. He was just about to say his last prayer, when barking dogs coming in from someplace drew the attention of the alpha male and the other gray. They suddenly turned and took flight. Fred just lay there for a few moments, watching the wolves scramble and disappear over a frozen hill, not fully believing he was still alive. But his ankle was bleeding through his boots. "Shit!"

He managed to sit up just in time to see six huskies running for all they were worth after the two wolves. He figured the ranger wasn't too far behind with the rest of his dogs. He knew beyond any doubt now that he should have stayed with Doug. He touched his jaw with his gloved hand. Bright blood oozed from the wound. He figured it needed several stitches, but he wasn't going to get them around here. He grabbed some snow and held it to his face to slow down the bleeding. At least, he hoped it would. The ankle would have to wait.

He was still alive, and his business wasn't finished. He heaved himself up and, with a renewed energy from knowing he'd survived almost certain death, trudged onward, passing an old, pieced-together truck, obviously made from parts of different vehicles. It looked abandoned, left off the road. It struck him then that he'd seen it on the way out with Doug. He had to be close to the cabin now! Had to be! And there was something else. Maybe it was just his imagination – cold playing with his brain – but he was certain there was something about that old truck that was very familiar, but he couldn't place it at the moment. He figured it didn't matter, anyway. An abandoned truck was of no use to him. He considered that more than likely it had broken down.

Indian Joe had barely let out a groan as Shelton went about removing the bullet from his side. Jenny stood to one side, looking on inquisitively, and Lois stood on the far end of the sofa, and handed Shelton towels and make-shift, surgical tools she'd managed to gather from the kitchen. They'd sterilized the wound with alcohol, reminding Lois of old western movies when whiskey was used for such antiquated surgeries. But it was all they had, and something had to be done. She happened to have some Neosporin in her medicine cabinet that had never been opened. That she had set aside for Shelton to put around the wound when he finished.

Joe winced as Shelton took one last dig in the wound with some long tweezers that Lois had previously taken out of her makeup bag and sterilized, and brought out the bullet. "Here it is!" he said, letting it drop with a thunk on the coffee table. "Mission accomplished." He then applied pressure on the open wound for a couple of minutes while Lois stacked a couple of white washcloths together and readied some medical tape, the kind you could tear off. Shelton then drew back the blood-soaked clothes and cleaned off around the side of the wound with alcohol on cotton balls, applied the Neosporin generously, and then laid clean washcloths on the wound and taped them down, wrapping tape around Joe's torso, to make sure it held. He asked Joe if he was okay. The Indian removed the cloth from his mouth that he'd been biting on and said he was.

"Good!" Shelton stood, stretching his arms out, and then pulling them back in quickly with a groan, having hurt his sore side. "I think I could use some coffee. What do you say, Indian? Think you could stand a cup?"

"I think so," Joe replied and then shut his eyes.

"I'll bring you some in a few minutes. Just you rest for a bit."

Joe nodded but didn't open his eyes.

Lois looked at Jenny who was taking it all in but not uttering a word. The redhead then laughed sardonically and went off to the bedroom and closed the door. It was apparent that she thought Shelton was nuts for helping Joe. Lois then sat down in a chair close to Joe, while Shelton made fresh coffee.

Jenny was pissed! She felt betrayed by Shelton, though she was the one who had betrayed him. Now he was helping these fools! She figured it inevitable that Shelton was going to do his best to fully charm these people over to his side and succeed in placing all blame on her and Fred. And that just wasn't gonna fly. Not now! Not ever! She sprawled across the bed, needing time to think, to plan what to do.

Doug knew of a short-cut that was off the road but through the woods which eventually trailed behind his cabin. Also, he was aware that if anyone was searching for him, they wouldn't see him if he did take that cut; but he figured it was worth it, if he had any chance at all in reaching the cabin before Fred.

Six of the dogs had taken off running earlier, apparently hearing something that Doug didn't, and three others had run off a few minutes prior to that to investigate something else, but when the rest, stirred up and excited, behaved as though they might leave, Nook swirled around and barked menacingly, letting them know he meant business, and they stayed behind.

Doug's hands and feet smarted from the cold, and he just knew his toes had frostbite. There wasn't anything he could do about it at that moment. He'd put on his sunglasses when the sun had come out for it's short visit, but it was growing dark again, and he'd had to remove them. The daylight had given his eyes a rest from the stinging cold. He'd been grateful for that. By the time he reached the trees off the road, the sun had fully set.

It was good dark now, and Fred's jaw hurt unbearably. The severely low temperature wasn't helping. He touched a gloved hand to the wound, swollen big time. "Damn wolf!" he snipped. "Wish I had his hide. I'd make him into a fur coat real quick." A much stronger wind-blast than any he'd previously suffered caught him off guard and sent him flying headlong into the snow. He lay there briefly, realizing his nostrils were full of ice and he couldn't breath. He managed to pull to his feet, snorting out the frozen snow and gasping for air through his mouth, which he could no longer feel, nor his nose. "Shit!"

It hit him that he no longer had his rifle. "Crap!" he scanned around, he could see in the darkness some, eyes having adjusted, but he didn't see the rifle, not even an indention in the snow – anywhere! "Not thinking clearly," he grumbled to himself. "Just not thinking clearly. Must have dropped it somewhere along the line. This cold is affecting my thinking, my reasoning, got to get out of this friggin' cold. Got to!"

Lois gave Joe some Tylenol PM that had been in the medicine cabinet for a couple of months but never had been opened. She'd almost forgotten about it, and was happy when she came across it while looking for something to help ease Joe's discomfort. At first, he'd refused, but when she insisted, he took two to make her happy. And he did fall asleep, and seemed to be resting easier than before.

Shelton, observing her as she stood over Joe, stated that she made one hell of a nurse. She thanked him, but said she was just doing what needed to be done. Just then, Jenny came out of the bedroom, wearing a strange expression. She said nothing, but went to the kitchen and could be heard getting herself a cup of coffee. Shelton and Lois shared dubious glances, and then Shelton nodded to Lois, indicating he was going into the kitchen. She shook her head that she understood and sat down beside Joe again.

"What you looking at?" Jenny quipped, as she finished pouring her coffee and leaned back against the sink.

"Something's going on in that head of yours. I can almost see the wheels turning under that red hair. And I'd wager it's not something good."

She simply smiled and took a sip of her coffee, eyeing him over the brim.

"Whatever you're thinking, you'd better forget it. There's enough trouble here."

"What? That you murdered a couple of old fogies and now you don't wanna pay for it? And Fred off and shot a ranger... Hey! I had nothing to do with any of them!"

"Maybe not directly, but indirectly, Jenny. This whole thing never would have taken place had it not been for your twisted thinking and scheming."

She guffawed. "Just what I thought. You're fuckin' gonna try to blame the entire thing on me!"

"No! Not all of it, Jenny. Still, you did start it! And you are guilty of swindling that poor old woman!"

"And you and Fred went right along with it." She suddenly turned and threw the mug down in the sink, breaking it into pieces, and then swung around, reached in her pocket and pulled out her 45, aiming it at Shelton's midsection.

He backed away instantly, knocking over a chair. "You crazy? What the hell you think you're doing?"

Realizing the sounds of things in the kitchen had grown serious; Lois jumped up and rushed to the kitchen. "Oh my God! Jenny! Put that thing away!"

Without taking her gray eyes off of Shelton, Jenny shook her head. "Hell no! Damn prick's plainly turned on me and Fred."

"It's no wonder," Lois said.

Jenny flashed angry eyes at Lois. "What the hell you mean, bitch?"

"You know... If you put that damn gun away and had the guts to take on a fair fight, I believe I could beat the crap out of you."

"Ha! You think so?"

"I *know* so!"

Jenny shook her head. "I ain't falling for that one, Lois. I know I could whip your frail little *pioneering* ass anytime – anyplace. You just don't want your new friend shot."

"I don't want *anyone* shot! Enough people have been killed and wounded here. Put that damn thing away!"

"Now the little missy is swearing. What'd ya know? You're talking mighty big to be on the hurtful end of a forty-five."

"Don't you threaten her," Shelton snarled.

"You gonna stop me, big man?"

Then, just as she said it, Shelton suddenly had her by the wrist, twisting her arm. She screamed out and the gun went off, but the bullet went through the ceiling. Shelton twisted her arm around to her back and, with his free arm, unbuckled his belt and secured her arms behind her. He shoved the very pissed off Jenny into the living room then and threw her down on the chair. "Yes!" he answered her question. "I am gonna stop you!"

The commotion had awoken Joe. He sat up, and it was obvious he hadn't missed much. He just kept his locked eyes on Jenny.

"What?" she said, glaring at the Indian.

"Things have a way of coming around," he stated flatly.

"Yeah... right," she responded and looked away.

"Sorry about that," Shelton said, having returned to the kitchen where Lois was standing looking out the window into the night. He was holding his side that was still giving him hell.

She turned around. "I just thank God no one got hurt."

"You're a good woman... And thanks."

"For what?"

"For challenging her. That was a brave thing to do. Jenny is one mean woman."

"What do you mean? I was serious. I can whip her!"

He studied her expression briefly and then broke into a grin and shook his head. "I believe you could...You're really something else, woman. Just wish you were mine – But," he put up a hand, "I understand you're not. And I respect you and your husband enough to know not to even try. Just wish I hadn't screwed my life up so damn awful. Getting to know you has given me the realization that there are good people in this world... Good women. Wish it weren't too late for me."

"It's not, Shelton! It's really not. You might have to spend some time in jail, but Joe and I will do all we can to help you. And I am sure Doug will listen to me – either one of us – and take what we have to say into consideration. That I promise!"

"Thank you kindly, Lois. I believe you. I'm just not sure, though. Just not sure."

"Well, think about it, anyway. Please!"
"I will... I will."

Doug finally reached the trees, thankful his heavy-duty flashlight was still working, for it was pitch dark inside the heavily wooded area, which he was fully aware went on for miles. He'd lived there for years, though, and had spent many hours hunting there in the same woods. He figured that if circumstances rendered it necessary he could probably make it through without the flashlight, but that would be appreciably difficult if it were not for the dogs, especially Nook, who seemed not to be deterred by his previous wound, and maintained a steady pace just a few feet ahead. Harbor was at his right side, and Shield, at his left. The rest of the dogs were in and out, still managing to keep up, but wandering off here and there from time to time. He figured they were the only ones who had actually enjoyed their trek across this frozen wilderness.

Inside the thick, piney woods, the snowfall was greatly thinned, not descending nearly as heavily, being braked by the thick limbs and branches overhead. And the snow wasn't quite as deep, but was still high and dense enough to warrant keeping the snowshoes on.

His face was so numb now; he kept touching it almost subconsciously, assuring himself that he still had one. He was like a person running the Boston Marathon, driven to the limits of exhaustion, but somehow, drawing up a renewed energy to push on even harder, that miraculous sudden burst of energy that all good athletes are fully familiar with. He surmised it was due to the knowledge that he was getting close to home, and he was growing more and more anxious to see if his wife was okay... and Joe. Had the Indian been able to rescue Lois? Or had that gone down badly? He prayed not. Onward, he pushed.

Chapter Nine

Fred stopped, his frosty breath streaming out in front of his face. That was it – Yellow light shown from the cabin up ahead. He was at the crest of a hill, and it was down hill all the way now. He took a step forward, moving a little too fast and slipped, causing him to fall and tumble two-thirds of the way down, losing one of his snowshoes in the process. But he didn't care now. He was there! Just another hundred yards and he'd be at the cabin!

Nikki raised his head and woofed. "What is it, Nikki?" Lois said, looking down at her dog that was lying at her feet under the kitchen table. Nikki stood and hastened into the living room to the front door, turning his face towards Lois as she joined him there. He woofed again. "Do you just want out?" she asked the dog, but believing it was more than a simple need to answer nature's call. "Someone out there?" This time he let out a sharp, quick bark, which answered her question. "Okay."

Shelton came up behind her. "What's going on?"

"Someone's coming. I'm sure of it."

"Think it's Doug?"

She rolled her eyes up and shook her head slightly. "Not sure. Don't think so. Not the way Nikki's acting. He's not wagging his tail, but he is excited."

"Maybe he just wants out?"

"No. That's not it. He'd be scratching and doing his potty dance. He's not doing that. No. Someone's out there."

Unbeknownst to them, Jenny had been working her hands behind her back, slowly slipping out of the belt's tight grip. She was almost free, but she kept silent, glancing over at Joe, who was still very sound asleep. A slight but definite smile came to her face as she freed herself and let the belt ease out of her fingers and fall softly to the floor. She kept her hands behind her back, giving the impression that they were still bound.

"Okay. Tell you what," Shelton said, speaking softly. "Put the dog in your bedroom. Otherwise, he might get hurt. And we don't want that."

"Right," Lois agreed, grabbing Nikki by his collar and taking him to her room, shoving him inside, as he didn't want to go, and closed the door. By then, Shelton was signaling, nodding his head, indicating for her to follow him on into the kitchen. She did as he suggested, and sat down to the table, while he poured more coffee in their cups.

"Just act natural," he said. "Make whoever it is think we haven't a clue."
She bobbed her head in acknowledgement.

In the living room, Jenny, eyes fixed on Joe, was making sure he was staying asleep, watching him anxiously, having caught a glimpse of Fred – and she was certain it was him now – as he'd passed in front of the light shining from the living-room to the front porch. There was a faint click, clicking. Fred was trying the door, but it was locked. Her eyes darted towards the kitchen and then back to the door. She took the chance and jumped up, rushing over and unlatching the door and letting Fred inside.

Chairs flew backwards as Shelton and Lois jumped up from the table, hearing the rush of wind coming from the front door. The expression in Shelton's green eyes said it all. This was it – The showdown! Off in the bedroom, Nikki barked feverishly, growling and scratching at the door.

Lois had never known such terror. There was an indescribable lump in her throat, as Shelton pulled the gun out of his belt, and pushed her back with his free arm and stood erect beside the refrigerator, waiting for Fred or Jenny to come around the corner.

In the living room, Fred indicated with a nod of his head sideways at Joe, who still appeared deep in sleep.

"He's no problem," Jenny whispered. "Just had a bullet removed, and he's knocked out with Tylenol PM."

"Sure?"

She nodded in the affirmative.

"I don't trust anyone, especially no Indian!" He said, still speaking very softly where she could barely hear and moved over to the sofa and stared down at Joe, who appeared to be knocked out cold. Fred poked him in the side with the nose of his gun, but the

Indian didn't even flinch. Fred looked back at Jenny and indicated for her to keep an eye on him. He then dug in his pocket and brought out a .22 and handed it over to Jenny.

She eagerly took the gun and grinned like a Cheshire cat.

Fred's eyes turned to the doorway of the kitchen. Slowly, he eased one foot in front of the other, keeping as snug to the wall as humanly possible.

The tension in the room could have been cut with a sword. Shelton shot Lois a glance and then turned his attention back to Fred, who was suddenly around the corner. Both men fired. Shelton caught a bullet in the right side of his chest. And Fred got it in the left shoulder. Lois, unsure of how serious Shelton's wound was, suddenly grabbed her cast-iron pot that was on the range and swung around, clobbering Fred as hard as she could, hitting him on his wounded side. Both men crumpled to the floor.

Jenny forgot about Joe and was in the kitchen and held her gun on Jenny. "Put the dammed thing down! Now! Or you're a goner, bitch!"

Defiantly, Lois stared at her. No way, did she want to let this woman win. She stood her ground.

"I said *now!*" Jenny yelled.

Joe was suddenly there, snatching the gun out of her hand and wrapping his free arm around her throat from behind and pulling her back, gun in her ribs.

"Mother fucker!" Jenny screeched.

But Fred, who wasn't wounded all that badly, regained his feet behind Joe and knocked him out with the butt of his gun.

Shelton looked up at Lois, eyes apologetic. "Sorry, fine lady. This is not what I intended at all."

"No!" She dropped to her knees. "Don't you dare die on me!"

But Jenny grabbed her by her hair and yanked her up. "Stay away from my husband!"

"You don't give a damn about him! He's hurt! Possibly dying! And you don't even care!"

"Damn right! But you tried to take him from me. No bitch takes my man from me, whether I want him or not!"

"Let it go, Jenny!" Fred said. "Shelton's hurt. Let her tend to him."

"Hell no!"

Ignoring Jenny, Fred stooped down in front of his former friend. "I'm sorry, Shelton. I never meant this, either. But it was you or me. I'm sorry about two-timing you with Jenny. I know now that she's no good. I should have seen it. However, like you, I was sucked in by her charm."

Shelton only faintly nodded that he understood, but he wasn't feeling too well. He closed his eyes.

"What the hell?" Jenny yelled.

"Just telling the truth," Fred stated, rising to his feet. "You're a cold-hearted bitch. I now wish I'd never let you talk me into turning on Shelton."

"How dare you!"

The .22 was lying in the middle of the kitchen floor where it had dropped from Joe's hand. The women eyed it at the same time and dove for it simultaneously. Both managed to get their hands on it, but lost grip in their mad struggle. They rolled around in the floor, clawing and hitting, screaming, biting and pulling hair. Lois managed to clip Jenny in the jaw, and Jenny, in turn, gave Lois a black eye.

Fred stood over the women as they fought like two alley cats. Question was – Was he going to take Jenny with him? It didn't take him long to decide. He bent over and grabbed both women by their hair and yanked them to their feet. He noticed that the Indian was regaining consciousness. That was when it hit Fred what was familiar about that abandoned truck. He'd seen that Indian driving it around Cold Town the day they had arrived. The unusual appearance of the old truck had struck him then. Why in hell hadn't he thought of it before now? "That truck down the road," he said to Joe, who was staring up at him now, from a sitting position. "It's yours, isn't it?"

Joe nodded that it was.

"Give me the damn keys!"

"Can't do that," Joe replied.

"Give me the damn keys, or I'll hot-wire it and take Lois with me."

Joe glared up at him with obsidian eyes, but reached in his pocket and dug out a set of keys with an eagle feather attached and handed them up to Fred, who let go of Lois.

"Better! Now, I'll take Jenny with me. And we're gonna leave you three here," he said, indicating to Shelton and Lois.

"The man needs help," Joe said, meaning Shelton. "He's could die soon, if he doesn't get medical attention."

"Too bad. It's him or me." He met eyes with Shelton who was wearing an unreadable expression. "I really do hate to do this to you, old friend. But I can't stick around any longer." He turned to Jenny. "Get your coat and let's get out of here."

Jenny was all for that, wasting no time in shrugging into her coat and grabbing her blue blanket. "You still got your share of the money?" she asked Fred.

"Yep! What's it to you?"

"Just wanted to make sure you still had it. That's all."

"Yeah... right."

"I want you to have your cut," she said, obviously trying to sound sincere.

He sniggered.

She ignored his response and headed for the door and opened it, waiting for Fred. Fred grabbed the weapons up, hoping to not leave any behind, and they backed out, slamming the door and making a run for it, bracing the biting snow and wind.

The only concerns Lois had now were wishing her husband were home and worrying about Shelton. She and Joe, with a hand over his own wound, rushed over to him and squatted down. He looked at them with strained eyes but said nothing.

Outside, Jenny yelled sideways at Fred, "My God! We'll never make it through this awful stuff!"

"You wanted outta there, didn't you?"

"Damn right!"

"Shut your face then. The Indian's truck is just up the road a piece. It appears to be especially built for rugged terrain and weather."

"Yeah?"

"Yep! I got this notion that it's not stuck at all. I think the Indian just wanted people to think it was. So, we're gonna take our chances."

"What if it really is?"

"We'll worry about that when the time comes. Now get your ass in gear and move it!"

"What you limping for?"

"Tangled with a couple of wolves back a ways. They got the worst end of the deal, though. Two of them dead now. Won't be tangling with anyone else."

"Y-You did?" she asked, starting to stutter from the cold.

"Yep! But we ain't got time to talk about it now."

"Ju-Just curious."

Doug was much closer to the cabin, instantly recognizing much of the brush and trees surrounding him and the dogs, most of which had returned. He was exhausted, anxious and short of breath, panting heavily, but he had to keep going. Had to! Nook was limping a little now; Doug realized the wound was starting to bother his best dog. He hoped he could tend to Nook's injury soon, before it became seriously infected.

There was a howling off in the distance, the wolves again. Nook turned his fine head to the left, in the direction the howling had come from, but he didn't let it slow down his pace, neither did the others. They seemed almost as anxious as Doug now to get home.

Breathing heavily, Doug encouraged Nook and the rest of the team onward. "Almost there, Nook... All of you. Almost there."

From the beam of his searchlight – off in the distance – Billy saw what appeared to be a couple of dead wolves lying in the snow. He shut off his Silverado and went to investigate. It was good dark now, though it was still fairly early. Not yet seven. He examined the bodies. One's skull was crushed in. No animal had done that. The weapon had been something hard, a piece of wood or the butt of a gun, probably a rifle. They'd tangled with a human. Probably one of the criminals. There was a trail of dark droplets, blood, leading away from the wolves. Whoever it was, had survived the struggle and walked away, and it looked as though they were headed for Doug's. It couldn't be Doug, for Doug had his dogs with him. Some of them, anyway. And there were no dog prints in the snow, which would have been smaller than the wolves. And none of the prints followed the human tracks. He had to assume the person was one of the killers. He hopped back in his vehicle and headed for Doug's.

"Lois! This is BP1... You there? Over."

Billy's voice was loud and clear. Lois looked into Shelton's drained face. "I should answer that. You need help!"

"Go ahead. Too late for me, kind lady. But for yourself and Indian Joe there," he said, indicating to Joe with a nod.

She jumped up and grabbed up the receiver. "Roger that! Lois here! I have a couple of injured men, Billy. One's really serious. Joe hurt too, but we got the bullet out. He's better... but still needs attention. Over."

"Roger! Okay... well... What about Doug? Is he there? Over."

She answered slowly. "Roger. No! No he's not. I haven't heard from him at all. Over."

"Copy. I think he's okay, Lois. Got reason to believe he may be headed your way. Anything else you want to tell me? Over."

"Roger! There's a man and a woman – Fred and Jenny. They left here. They have the keys to Joe's old truck. They intend to take it and flee. Over."

"Roger! Don't think they'll get far. So, you're okay? Over."

"Roger. But these two need medical attention ASAP. Over."

"Copy that. I'll get there as soon as I can. Over and out."

"Roger." She sat down the receiver and went back over to Shelton, who was smiling weakly. "Hang in there." Then softly added, "For me?"

He stared at her briefly and then his eyes filled with tears. "Since you put it that way, fine lady. I'll do my best."

About a half mile from the cabin, not seeing Fred and Jenny who were just over a hill, Doug could still make out the dark image of Joe's truck still sitting where it had been when he'd left with Fred. He'd soon know how that had turned out. He jerked his head to the right as a wolf howled. This time, it sounded much closer. Surely they weren't pursuing him and his dogs. Though the wolves were bigger, they were outnumbered by the huskies. Certainly they wouldn't try for him with the dogs again. He wondered if the natural predators were homing in on something or someone else. Maybe there was an injured animal about? Or was it Fred? He knew Fred had guns, but wolves were quick and very good at sneaking up on you. And a greenhorn like Fred would be relatively easy prey.

At last, Fred and Jenny finally reached the truck, and it took several attempts, but Fred finally got the old truck started up. "Thought so," he said to Jenny, who was sitting beside him, shivering so hard she was vibrating and making moaning sounds through her teeth.

"D-Damn g-goo-od th-thing!" she managed.

"Or what?" he asked, looking at her unflinchingly.

"I-It's our o-only ch-chance out of th-this G-God-forsaken p-place! That's wh-hat!"

He sniggered.

"Wh-What the fu-fuck d-d you th-think is s-so f-funny?"

"You! You sitting there talking so big. Should say – trying to talk. But you're really in no position at all to talk big now, are you?"

Something flickered in her eyes, a look of uneasiness. "Wh-What do you-you m-mean by th-that?"

"Just what I said." He turned his eyes to the windshield. "It's gonna take forever for that damn snow to melt off there enough for me to see. Gonna have to help it along." He flashed her an ambiguous smile and opened the door. "Now you just sit tight there, sweetie... until we get this old truck warmed up and ready to go."

Twisting her mouth around, looking a bit uncertain, she nodded.

He grinned hugely at her expression, and then got out and went to cleaning off the windows.

"Shelton?" Lois cried out, realizing he was unconscious. *"Shelton?"*

Joe had been in the kitchen making more coffee, he hurried in, stooped down and felt Shelton's pulse. "He's still alive, Lois."

"Thank God!"

"You really like him, don't you, Lois?"

"I believe he really isn't a bad person. I think he just made some very bad mistakes. Still, you know as well as I. He's not really mean."

"But he did kill Clifford and Bell," he reminded her.

"He didn't mean to. He was trapped in a situation and panicked. And it just accelerated from there, got worse and worse."

Joe nodded in agreement. "Yes. It is unfortunate. But, if he lives he will have to pay for his mistakes."

"I know that, Joe. But I promised him that I... That we'd tell the truth. He has made every effort to turn around these last few hours. You know. You've been here."

He only had to think about it a moment. "Yes, ma'am. I surely will tell the truth. I just hope he makes it."

"He'd got to! He's got to!" A tear slid down her cheek.

Joe touched her face with his fingertips and gently removed the tear, and then he stood and went back in kitchen and poured her a fresh cup of coffee and brought it to her. She thanked him and just sat down beside Shelton in the floor, wanting to be there for him.

Fred jumped back in the truck, glanced over at Jenny, whose teeth were still chattering. "Not cold, are you?" She gave him a dark scowl, and he guffawed. He then turned his attention to getting them out of the rut. It took a few tries of backing up and then pulling forward, but the tires were large and chained, and soon he had the vehicle free. "Whoopee! We're out!" he yelled and smiled smugly at Jenny.

"J-Just get us the f-fuck out of this frozen hell," she said, fixing her eyes on the frozen-over-road ahead. "I'll *never* come back here! Not for love nor money!"

He sniggered, still staring ahead, doing his best to make out the road between the wiper swipes. "Now for love, I might believe you. But – for money? Knowing you, I wouldn't be so quick to say you'd never come back for money."

"Not even for money!" she maintained.

He glanced at her long enough to cock his head, indicating that he wasn't so sure.

"Never!"

He chortled and eased his foot down on the gas pedal. "Let's get this show on the road!"

Just up a ways, two wolves passed in his headlights. "Damn! If that ain't the mother-fuckers that attacked me!"

"Crap! I had no idea they were *that* big!" Jenny stated.

"Sure ain't Chihuahuas."

"No they aren't. They're fucking huge!"

"I'm damn lucky to be alive. If I hadn't had my rifle with me, I wouldn't be."

"Yeah... guess so," Jenny said, watching the glowing eyes of the black wolf eying her, as he lead the gray to the far side of the road. "Damn! Their eyes are eerie!" '

"You should have seen the white one... an albino. His eyes were red when the light was on them."

"Really? That would really freak me out."

"What's scary is their friggin' fangs coming at your throat."

"Yeah. I suppose that would be very scary."

Headlights were coming Billy's way from the opposing direction. "What the?" He couldn't believe it. Someone was out driving in this. He strained his neck forward, trying to make out what kind of vehicle it was. "I'll be a monkey's uncle!" he yelled, as the truck passed. "That's Indian Joe's truck!" He slammed his fist on the steering wheel. There was no doubt then that the person driving it was one of the thugs he was after. He quickly eased down on his brakes, doing his best not to slide off what was perceived to be the road and slowly began turning his Silverado around. There was a precipice not too far off the side that paralleled the highway. That was one thing that blatantly reminded him where the road was. No way did he want to go sailing over that. He'd be hamburger mixed with shredded metal if they ever found him at all. It was a five-thousand-foot drop at the very least. It took him four tries, but he finally got righted around and headed back the other direction. He couldn't see any red tail lights up ahead, but knew they were probably just over a hill. They couldn't have gone too far.

"What are you doing?" Jenny asked, for Fred suddenly stopped the truck by what she considered an iffy spot near the edge of a cliff. They'd passed a sign a few seconds before that said *Ryan's Lookout.* Though snow-covered, there'd been a place to pull off there. There wasn't one here. What was his reasoning? She couldn't tell how far down it went, it was too dark.

"You'll see." He opened his door and got out, walking around to her side. Her eyes were glued to his now unreadable face as he opened her door.

"Get out."

"What? You crazy? Let's go! I just want to get outta here!"

"Me too. Only you ain't going with me."

Her eyes were instant saucers of fright as the realization of his intentions hit her. *"Hell no!"* she screamed and tried to slam the door, but he held it fast, yanking it back open with such force that she flew out and down, sliding to where her face was only inches away from the edge of the cliff. He then slammed the door shut, pushed the button on the key fob and the doors locked. Quickly, pawing snow from off her face and crying uncontrollably, she desperately scrambled around and to her feet and reached in desperation for the door, but he kicked her back hard, leaving her teetering momentarily, arms flailing, fighting with all she had to keep from falling backwards, but lost the struggle and fell screaming over the cliff.

"That'll teach you, bitch!" He said, staring over the precipice. He knew it had to be a long way down, for he counted twenty slow seconds before the end of her screaming and all was silent again. He then spit over the cliff.

Realizing headlights were headed his way, he swiftly turned, unlocked the doors and jumped back in the truck and took off, once more going back towards the cabin, knowing it had to be the vehicle he had passed only minutes before. He'd wondered then if it was a police vehicle of some kind. It had one of those long radio antennas. He gestured the bird at the ranger as he passed by again. "Catch me... if you can, ranger?" He was feeling more confident now in Joe's truck. He was moving away from the precipice and felt it was no longer a threat and gave the truck more gas. He went a couple of miles, knowing he was driving too fast for the conditions, but he wanted to lose that ranger. He wheeled around a curb and slammed on his brakes as another moose was suddenly in the beam of his headlights, smack in the middle of his path. The truck went hurtling, spinning around five times before slamming to a stop against a mound of frozen snow. *"Jeez!"* He sat there stunned for several minutes, before realizing he had a bloody mouth and swelling bottom lip from bouncing his face off the steering wheel. He spit blood and then, with some effort, as the door was bent slightly, he opened it. The ranger's headlights were shining around the curve. He started running the best he could in the deep snow. This time there were no snowshoes.

Fred ran like hell in a diagonal line, cutting a path across and away from the highway, for what seemed to be an eternity, with the ranger still following along the road in his vehicle. For once,

Fred was thankful for the snow. Otherwise, the man might have caught up with him.

Once more, the cabin was in view. There was no other choice. He headed directly for the cabin. He knew Lois was still there with two injured men. He'd take the woman for hostage if he had to.

Harbor barked first, and then Shield, and soon the rest were barking excitedly, including Nook, in spite of Doug's trying to keep them quiet. Something was happening.

He was drawing near the cabin when he saw a flash of headlights coming around the curve up ahead. As he moved closer to the front of the trees where the back of his property began, he noticed the tall figure of a man running as hard as he could for the conditions. It had to be one of the crooks.

Shelton was still passed out, and Joe was in the bathroom cleaning up when the commotion began. Lois ran to the front door, opened it and looked out. What appeared to be a man was running towards the cabin. Was it Doug? She rushed across the porch and out into the snow, leaving Nikki inside. But he was barking menacingly. Wasn't Doug! More dogs were barking out back. They sounded familiar. Just then, the headlights caught the man's face enough for her to see it was Fred returning. And he was running for all he was worth and yelling at her.

"Oh God!" she turned to run back inside, but she tripped and he was upon her, grabbing her by the arm, shoving the nose of a gun in her side. Just then, Nook and the rest of the dogs scuttled around the corner of the cabin, Doug behind them, and they would have attacked Fred, but stopped in their tracks when they saw Lois standing there. Doug yelled at them as he instantly surmised the situation. *"Easy... boys!"*

"Doug!" she cried, tears of absolute terror in her eyes. The dogs circled around them, lips curled, growling low.

"Get them away!" Fred ordered. "Or she's a dead woman!"

Billy suddenly swung his vehicle in the drive and jumped out. Doug yelled that Fred had a gun on Lois, not to move.

"What are you gonna accomplish? It's over," Doug said.

"Wh-Where's Jenny?" Lois asked.

"That fickle little slut? Let's say she's taking a long nap."

As soon as Joe heard the commotion, he looked out the front window. Shelton moaned, opened his eyes and was now conscience. He asked Joe what was up. Joe told him that Fred was back, had Lois and was threatening her with a gun.

"That fucking bastard!" Shelton said; face crimson, mustering all his strength to stand. "He'd better not hurt that nice little lady."

"Don't look good," Joe said, not aware that Shelton had made it into the kitchen and was heading out the back door. He turned around and realized Shelton was no longer standing behind him. "Where'd he go?" Then he heard the back door close. "Crazy man!" Joe was afraid Shelton would just aggravate an already bad situation. He followed out the back, but Shelton had disappeared into the darkness. How could such a seriously injured man move so quickly?

Outside, Fred was dragging Lois around in circles, not really knowing what he was going to do. Neither ranger dared move towards him, afraid he'd kill Lois. He decided to start backing away.

"Where you going?" Doug yelled. "Lois doesn't even have on a coat!"

"That's the least of her worries, ranger." Fred said, continuing to walk backwards. "Toss me your keys, ranger," he yelled at Billy.

"Hell no!"

Fred jabbed the gun in Lois' side, causing her to yell out.

"All right!' Billy tossed him the keys, just as he did, he noticed a man slipping behind the Silverado. At first, he thought it might be Joe, but he appeared taller, and then Joe was there, too. But Billy kept quiet, and so did Doug, whose eyes were fixed on his wife, and looking profoundly helpless.

Fred continued stepping backwards, pulling Lois along with him. She was crying and telling Doug she loved him. Fred yelled at her to keep her mouth shut as they reached the passenger side of the truck. He had to let go of her long enough to open the door to the cab. And just as he did, she made an effort to run away. He spun around and ordered her to stop or he'd shoot. She did, instantly, standing their rigid and panting, afraid to move, back turned to Fred.

"Just do as he says, Lois," Doug said. "Just do as he says." But his eyes steadied on the two men whose presence Fred wasn't aware.

She bobbed her head that she would and sucked in air.

Fred suddenly yelled and Lois heard struggling behind her and realized Fred had dropped his gun. Then Joe stepped out where she could see him. She swung around to see what was happening. Shelton had his belt around Fred's throat and was pulling as tight as he could. Fred clawed at Shelton's hands with all his might for several seconds, but soon lost the battle. When he got still, Shelton just let him drop to the ground, then fell back, winded, against the truck. "That'll teach you to hurt such a nice lady as Lois," he mumbled.

Relieved, Lois ran to Doug with open arms, hugging and kissing him and babbling about what had happened. He asked her to slow down so he could understand her. She did. The dogs were running around excitedly, sniffing at Fred's body and barking. Billy and Joe went up to Shelton, who wasn't looking so good. "Come on, friend," Joe said. "We need to get you into Cold Town... Get you some help."

"No," Shelton said and looked over at the now happy couple. "I'll never make it that far."

Lois heard, and backing away from her husband, spun around and ran over to Shelton. "Please! For my sake, Shelton. Please!"

"What have I got to live for, anyway?" he said, looking at her kindly.

"You can find yourself someone like me," she said.

"Kind lady, there's not another like you."

"I won't argue that," Doug agreed, stepping up. "But Lois just told me that you've done everything you could to try and right things. What's even more important, you just saved her life. You'd better bet we'll do all we can to help you."

"I... I don't know, ranger."

"You have to try, Shelton!" Lois insisted.

"Okay... for you..." With that, he smiled slightly and nodded, then passed out and slid to the ground. Doug and Billy lifted him up and put him in the truck. Joe hastened inside and quickly grabbed some blankets, hurried back out, tossed one in for Shelton and then climbed in the back.

"I'm calling Doctor Pocius now and letting him know you're on your way," Doug said.

Billy nodded, started up the truck and backed out. Doug and Lois waited on the porch until the truck was headed down the road. "Notice something?" he said, craning his neck and looking skyward. "There's not a cloud in the sky now!"

She looked up too. He was right. The stars were out so bright and clear it looked as though one could reach out and touch them. "Absolutely beautiful!"

"One of the things I love about it here," he said. "Now, I guess we'd better go call the doctor. I'll feed and water the dogs after that. Tomorrow... I'll start working on getting the truck and sled back. Hope Joe's up to helping me."

"I think he will be. He's a tough old Indian."

"That he definitely is. And I just know he's beating himself up because he feels he wasn't the help he wanted to be."

"He was here. That's what counts. He did his best. Not his fault things went crazy."

"And I told him so."

Then, with concern in her face, she looked up to her husband. "You think Shelton will make it?"

"I hope so, Lois. I sure hope so. He saved your life... and he may very well have saved Joe's."

With that, he gave her a gentle squeeze and they walked in the house, dogs rushing in ahead. They seemed to know everything was going to be all right now.

Early the next morning Jasper called in for Billy to let them know that Shelton would make it. And that Joe had left the hospital and was on his way out.

The end